DANDELION COTTAGE

CARROLL WATSON RANKIN

First published in 1904

ISBN-13: 978-1539946175
ISBN-10: 1539946177

CONTENTS

CHAPTER 1.
MR. BLACK'S TERMS

The little square cottage was unoccupied. It had stood for many years on the parish property, having indeed been built long before the parish bought the land for church purposes. It was easy to see how Dandelion Cottage came by its name at first, for growing all about it were great, fluffy, golden dandelions; but afterwards there was another good reason why the name was appropriate, as you will discover shortly.

The cottage stood almost directly behind the big stone church in Lakeville, a thriving Northern Michigan town, and did not show very plainly from the street because it was so small by contrast with everything else near it. This was fortunate, because, after the Tuckers had moved into the big new rectory, the smaller house looked decidedly forlorn and deserted.

"We'll leave it just where it stands," the church wardens had said, many years previously. "It's precisely the right size for Doctor and Mrs. Gunn, for they would rather have a small house than a large one. When they leave us and we are selecting another clergyman, we'll try to get one with a small family."

This plan worked beautifully for a number of years. It succeeded so well, in fact, that the vestry finally forgot to be cautious, and when at last it secured the services of Dr. Tucker, the church had grown so used to clergymen with small families that the vestrymen engaged the new minister without remembering to ask if his family would fit Dandelion Cottage.

But when Dr. Tucker and Mrs. Tucker and eight little Tuckers, some on foot and some in baby carriages, arrived, the vestrymen regretted this oversight. They could see at a glance that the tiny cottage could never hold them all.

"We'll just have to build a rectory on the other lot," said Mr. Black, the senior warden. "That's all there is about it. The cottage is all out of repair, anyway. It wasn't well built in the first place, and the last three clergymen have complained bitterly of the inconvenience of having to hold up umbrellas in the different rooms every time it rained. Their wives objected to the wall paper and to being obliged to keep the potatoes in the bedroom closet. It's really time we had a new rectory."

"It certainly is," returned the junior warden, "and we'll all have to take turns entertaining all the little Tuckers that there isn't room for in the cottage while the new house is getting built."

Seven of the eight little Tuckers were boys. If it hadn't been for Bettie they would all have been boys, but Bettie saved the day. She was a slender twelve-year-old little Bettie, with big brown eyes, a mop of short brown curls, and such odd clothes. Busy Mrs. Tucker was so in the habit of making boys' garments that she could not help giving a boyish cut even to Bettie's dresses. There were always sailor collars to the waists, and the skirts were invariably kilted. Besides this, the little girl wore boys' shoes.

"You see," explained Bettie, who was a cheerful little body, "Tommy has to take them next, and of course it wouldn't pay to buy shoes for just one girl."

The little Tuckers were not the only children in the neighborhood. Bettie found a bosom friend in Dr. Bennett's Mabel, who lived next door to the rectory, another in Jeanie Mapes, who lived across the street, and still another in Marjory Vale, whose home was next door to Dandelion Cottage.

Jean, as her little friends best liked to call her, was a sweet-faced, gentle-voiced girl of fourteen. Mothers of other small girls were always glad to see their own more scatterbrained daughters tucked under Jean's loving wing, for thoroughly-nice Jean, without being in the least priggish, was considered a safe and desirable companion. It doesn't always follow that children like the persons it is considered best for them to like, but in Jean's case both parents and daughters agreed that Jean was not only safe but delightful—the charming daughter of a charming mother.

Marjory, a year younger and nearly a head shorter than Jean, often seemed older. Outwardly, she was a sedate small person, slight, blue-eyed, graceful, and very fair. Her manners at times were very pleasing, her self-possession almost remarkable; this was the result of careful training by a conscientious, but at that time sadly unappreciated, maiden aunt who was Marjory's sole guardian. There were moments, however, when Marjory, who was less sedate than she appeared, forgot to be polite. At such times, her ways were apt to be less pleasing than those of either Bettie or Jean, because her wit was nimbler, her tongue sharper, and her heart a trifle less tender. Her mother had died when Marjory was only a few weeks old, her father had lived only two years longer, and the rather solitary little girl had missed much of the warm family affection that had fallen to the lot of her three more fortunate friends. Those who knew her well found much in her to like, but among her schoolmates there were girls who said that Marjory was "stuck-up," affected, and "too smart."

Mabel, the fourth in this little quartet of friends, was eleven, large

for her age and young for her years, always an unfortunate combina-
tion of circumstances. She was intensely human and therefore liable
to err, and, it may be said, she very seldom missed an opportunity. In
school she read with a tremendous amount of expression but mispro-
nounced half the words; when questions were asked, she waved her
hand triumphantly aloft and gave anything but the right answer; she
had a surprising stock of energy, but most of it was misdirected. Warm-
hearted, generous, heedless, hot-tempered, and always blundering, she
was something of a trial at home and abroad; yet no one could help
loving her, for everybody realized that she would grow up some day
into a really fine woman, and that all that was needed in the meantime
was considerable patience. Rearing Mabel was not unlike the task of
bringing up a St. Bernard puppy. Mrs. Bennett was decidedly glad to
note the growing friendship among the four girls, for she hoped that
Mabel would in time grow dignified and sweet like Jean, thoughtful and
tender like Bettie, graceful and prettily mannered like Marjory. But this
happy result had yet to be achieved.

The little one-story cottage, too much out of repair to be rented,
stood empty and neglected. To most persons it was an unattractive spot
if not actually an eyesore. The steps sagged in a dispirited way, some
of the windows were broken, and the fence, in sympathy perhaps with
the house, had shed its pickets and leaned inward with a discouraged,
hopeless air.

But Bettie looked at the little cottage longingly—she could gaze right
down upon it from the back bedroom window—a great many times a day.
It didn't seem a bit too big for a playhouse. Indeed, it seemed a great pity
that such a delightful little building should go unoccupied when Bettie
and her homeless dolls were simply suffering for just such a shelter.

"Wouldn't it be nice," said Bettie, one day in the early spring, "if we
four girls could have Dandelion Cottage for our very own?"

"Wouldn't it be sweet," mimicked Marjory, "if we could have the moon and about twenty stars to play jacks with?"

"The cottage isn't quite so far away," said Jean. "It would be just lovely to have it, for we never have a place to play in comfortably."

"We're generally disturbing grown-ups, I notice," said Marjory, comically imitating her Aunty Jane's severest manner. "A little less noise, if you please. Is it really necessary to laugh so much and so often?"

"Even Mother gets tired of us sometimes," confided Jean. "There are days when no one seems to want all of us at once."

"I know it," said Bettie, pathetically, "but it's worse for me than it is for the rest of you. You have your rooms and nobody to meddle with your things. I no sooner get my dolls nicely settled in one corner than I have to move them into another, because the babies poke their eyes out. It's dreadful, too, to have to live with so many boys. I fixed up the cunningest playhouse under the clothes-reel last week, but the very minute it was finished Rob came home with a horrid porcupine and I had to move out in a hurry."

"Perhaps," suggested Marjory, "we could rent the cottage."

"Who'd pay the rent?" demanded Mabel. "My allowance is five cents a week and I have to pay a fine of one cent every time I'm late to meals."

"How much do you have left?" asked Jeanie, laughing.

"Not a cent. I was seven cents in debt at the end of last week."

"I get two cents a hundred for digging dandelions," said Marjory, "but it takes just forever to dig them, and ugh! I just hate it."

"I never have any money at all," sighed Bettie. "You see there are so many of us."

"Let's go peek in at the windows," suggested Mabel, springing up from the grass. "That much won't cost us anything at any rate."

Away scampered the four girls, taking a short cut through Bettie's back yard.

The cottage had been vacant for more than a year and had not improved in appearance. Rampant vines clambered over the windows and nowhere else in town were there such luxurious weeds as grew in the cottage yard. Nowhere else were there such mammoth dandelions or such prickly burrs. The girls waded fearlessly through them, parted the vines, and, pressing their noses against the glass, peered into the cottage parlor.

"What a nice, square little room!" said Marjory.

"I don't think the paper is very pretty," said Mabel.

"We could cover most of the spots with pictures," suggested practical Marjory.

"It looks to me sort of spidery," said Mabel, who was always somewhat pessimistic. "Probably there's rats, too."

"I know how to stop up rat holes," said Bettie, who had not lived with seven brothers without acquiring a number of useful accomplishments. "I'm not afraid of spiders—that is, not so very much."

"What are you doing here?" demanded a gruff voice so suddenly that everybody jumped.

The startled girls wheeled about. There stood Bettie's most devoted friend, the senior warden.

"Oh!" cried Bettie, "it's only Mr. Black."

"Were you looking for something?" asked Mr. Black.

"Yes," said Bettie. "We're looking for a house. We'd like to rent this one, only we haven't a scrap of money."

"And what in the name of common sense would you do with it?"

"We want it for our dolls," said Bettie, turning a pair of big pleading brown eyes upon Mr. Black. "You see, we haven't any place to play. Marjory's Aunty Jane won't let her cut papers in the house, so she can't have any paper dolls, and I can't play any place because I have so many brothers. They tomahawk all my dolls when they play Indian, shoot them with beans when they play soldiers, and drown them all when they play shipwreck. Don't you think we might be allowed to use the cottage if we'd promise to be very careful and not do any damage?"

"We'd clean it up," offered Marjory, as an inducement.

"We'd mend the rat holes," offered Jean, looking hopefully at Bettie.

"Would you dig the weeds?" demanded Mr. Black.

There was a deep silence. The girls looked at the sea of dandelions and then at one another.

"Yes," said Marjory, finally breaking the silence. "We'd even dig the weeds."

"Yes," echoed the others. "We'd even dig the weeds—and there's just millions of 'em."

"Good!" said Mr. Black. "Now, we'll all sit down on the steps and I'll tell you what we'll do. It happens that the Village Improvement Society has just notified the vestry that the weeds on this lot must be removed before they go to seed—the neighbors have complained about them. It would cost the parish several dollars to hire a man to do the work, and we're short of funds just now. Now, if you four girls will pull up every weed in this place before the end of next week you shall have the use of the cottage for all the rest of the summer in return for your services. How does that strike you?"

"Oh!" cried Bettie, throwing her arms about Mr. Black's neck. "Do let me hug you. Oh, I'm glad—glad!"

"There, there!" cried stout Mr. Black, shaking Bettie off and dropping her where the dandelions grew thickest. "I didn't say I was to be strangled as part of the bargain. You'd better save your muscle for the dandelions. Remember, you've got to pay your rent in advance. I shan't hand over the key until the last weed is dug."

"We'll begin this minute!" cried enthusiastic Mabel. "I'm going straight home for a knife."

CHAPTER 2.
PAYING THE RENT

"This is a whopping big yard," said Mabel, looking disconsolately at two dandelions and one burdock in the bottom of a bushel basket. "There doesn't seem to be any place to begin."

"I'm going to weed out a place big enough to sit in," announced Bettie. "Then I'll make it bigger and bigger all around me in every direction until it joins the clearing next to mine."

"I'm a soldier," said Marjory, brandishing a trowel, "vanquishing my enemies. You know in books the hero always battles single-handed with about a million foes and always kills them all and everybody lives happy ever after—zip! There goes one!"

"I'm a pioneer," said Jean, slashing away at a huge, tough burdock. "I'm chopping down the forest primeval to make a potato patch. The dandelions are skulking Indians, and I'm capturing them to put in my bushel-basket prison."

"I'm just digging weeds," said prosaic Mabel, "and I don't like it."

"Neither does anybody else," said Marjory, "but I guess having the cottage will be worth it. Just pretend it's something else and then you won't mind it so much. Play you're digging for diamonds."

"I can't," returned Mabel, hopelessly. "I haven't any imagination. This is just plain dirt and I can't make myself believe it's anything else."

By supper time the cottage yard presented a decidedly disreputable appearance. Before the weeds had been disturbed they stood upright, presenting an even surface of green with a light crest of dandelion gold. But now it was different. Although the number of weeds was not greatly decreased, the yard looked as if, indeed, a battle had been fought there. Mr. Black, passing by on his way to town, began to wonder if he had been quite wise in turning it over to the girls.

At four o'clock the following morning, sleepy Bettie tumbled out of bed and into her clothes. Then she slipped quietly downstairs, out of doors, through the convenient hole in the back fence, and into the cottage yard. She had been digging for more than an hour when Jean, rubbing a pair of sleepy eyes, put in her appearance.

"Oh!" cried Jean, disappointedly. "I meant to have a huge bare field to show you when you came, and here you are ahead of me. What a lot you've done!"

"Yes," assented Bettie, happily. "There's room for me and my basket, too, in my patch. I'll have to go home after a while to help dress the children."

Young though she was—she was only twelve—Bettie was a most helpful young person. It is hard to imagine what Mrs. Tucker would have done without her cheerful little daughter. Bettie always spoke of the boys as "the children," and she helped her mother darn their stockings, sew on their buttons, and sort out their collars. The care of the family baby, too, fell to her lot.

The boys were good boys, but they were boys. They were willing to do errands or pile wood or carry out ashes, but none of them ever thought of doing one of these things without first being told—sometimes they had to be told a great many times. It was different with Bettie.

If Tom ate crackers on the front porch, it was Bettie who ran for the broom to brush up the crumbs. If the second-baby-but-one needed his face washed—and it seemed to Bettie that there never was a time when he didn't need it washed—it was Bettie who attended to it. If the cat looked hungry, it was Bettie who gave her a saucer of milk. Dick's rabbits and Rob's porcupine would have starved if Bettie had not fed them, and Donald's dog knew that if no one else remembered his bone kind Bettie would bear it in mind.

The boys' legs were round and sturdy, but Bettie's were very much like pipe stems.

"I don't have time to get fat," Bettie would say. "But you don't need to worry about me. I think I'm the healthiest person in the house. At least I'm the only one that hasn't had to have breakfast in bed this week."

Neither Marjory nor Mabel appeared during the morning to dig their share of the weeds, but when school was out that afternoon they were all on hand with their baskets.

"I had to stay," said Mabel, who was the last to arrive. "I missed two words in spelling."

"What were they?" asked Marjory.

"'Parachute' and 'dandelion.' I hate dandelions, anyway. I don't know what parachutes are, but if they're any sort of weeds I hate them, too."

The girls laughed. Mabel always looked on the gloomiest side of things and always grumbled. She seemed to thrive on it, however, for she was built very much like a barrel and her cheeks were like a pair of round red apples. She was always honest, if a little too frank in expressing her opinions, and the girls liked her in spite of her blunt ways. She was the youngest of the quartet, being only eleven.

"There doesn't seem to be much grass left after the weeds are out," said Bettie, surveying the bare, sandy patch she had made.

"This has always been a weedy old place," replied Jean. "I think the whole neighborhood will feel obliged to us if we ever get the lot cleared. Perhaps our landlord will plant grass seed. It would be fine to have a lawn."

"Perhaps," said Marjory, "he'll let us have some flower beds. Wouldn't it be lovely to have nasturtiums running right up the sides of the house?"

"They'd be lovely among the vines," agreed Bettie. "I've some poppy seeds that we might plant in a long narrow bed by the fence."

"There are hundreds of little pansy plants coming up all over our yard," said Jean. "We might make a little round bed of them right here where I'm sitting. What are you going to plant in your bed, Mabel?"

"Butter-beans," said that practical young person, promptly.

"Well," said Bettie, with a long sigh, "we'll have to work faster than this or summer will be over before we have a chance to plant anything. This is the biggest little yard I ever did see."

For a time there was silence. Marjory, the soldier, fell upon her foes with renewed vigor, and soon had an entire regiment in durance vile. Jean, the pioneer, fell upon the forest with so much energy that its speedy extermination was threatened. Mabel seized upon the biggest and toughest burdock she could find and pulled with both hands and all her might, until, with a sharp crack, the root suddenly parted and Mabel, very much to her own surprise, turned a back somersault and landed in Bettie's basket.

"Hi there!" cried a voice from the road. "How are you youngsters getting along?"

The girls jumped to their feet—all but Mabel, who was still wedged tightly in Bettie's basket. There was Mr. Black, with his elbows on the fence, and with him was the president of the Village Improvement Society; both were smiling broadly.

"Sick of your bargain?" asked Mr. Black.

The four girls shook their heads emphatically.

"Hard work?"

Four heads bobbed up and down.

"Well," said Mr. Black, encouragingly, "you've made considerable headway today."

"Where are you putting the weeds?" asked the president of the Village Improvement Society.

"On the back porch in a piano box," said Bettie. "We had a big pile of them last night, but they shrank like everything before morning. If they do that every time, it won't be necessary for Mabel to jump on them to press them down."

"Let me know when you have a wagon load," said Mr. Black. "I'll have them hauled away for you."

For the rest of the week the girls worked early and late. They began almost at daylight, and the mosquitoes found them still digging at dusk.

By Thursday night, only scattered patches of weeds remained. The little diggers could hardly tear themselves away when they could no longer find the weeds because of the gathering darkness. Now that the task was so nearly completed it seemed such a waste of time to eat and sleep.

Bettie was up earlier than ever the next morning, and with one of the boys' spades had loosened the soil around some of the very worst patches before any of the other girls appeared.

By five o'clock that night the last weed was dug. Conscientious Bettie went around the yard a dozen times, but however hard she might search, not a single remaining weed could she discover.

"Good work," said Jean, balancing her empty basket on her head.

"It seems too good to be true," said Bettie, "but think of it, girls—the rent is paid! It's 'most time for Mr. Black to go by. Let's watch for him from the doorstep—our own precious doorstep."

"It needs scrubbing," said Mabel. "Besides, it isn't ours, yet. Perhaps

Mr. Black has changed his mind. Some grown-up folks have awfully changeable minds."

"Oh!" gasped Marjory. "Wouldn't it be perfectly dreadful if he had!"

It seemed to the little girls, torn between doubt and expectation, that Mr. Black was strangely indifferent to the calls of hunger that night. Was he never going home to dinner? Was he never coming?

"Perhaps," suggested Jean, "he has gone out of town."

"Or forgotten us," said Marjory.

"Or died," said Mabel, dolefully.

"No—no," cried Bettie. "There he is; he's coming around the corner now—I can see him. Let's run to meet him."

The girls scampered down the street. Bettie seized one hand, Mabel the other, Marjory and Jean danced along ahead of him, and everybody talked at once. Thus escorted, Mr. Black approached the cottage lot.

"Well, I declare," said Mr. Black. "You haven't left so much as a blade of grass. Do you think you could sow some grass seed if I have the ground made ready for it?"

The girls thought they could. Bettie timidly suggested nasturtiums.

"Flower beds too? Why, of course," said Mr. Black. "Vegetables as well if you like. You can have a regular farm and grow fairy beanstalks and Cinderella pumpkins if you want to. And now, since the rent seems to be paid, I suppose there is nothing left for me to do but to hand over the key. Here it is, Mistress Bettie, and I'm sure I couldn't have a nicer lot of tenants."

CHAPTER 3.
THE TENANTS TAKE POSSESSION

"Our own house—think of it!" cried Bettie, turning the key. "Push, somebody; the door sticks. There! It's open."

"Ugh!" said Mabel, drawing back hastily. "It's awfully dark and stuffy in there. I guess I won't go in just yet—it smells so dead-ratty."

"It's been shut up so long," explained Jean. "Wait. I'll pull some of the vines back from this window. There! Can you see better?"

"Lots," said Bettie. "This is the parlor, girls—but, oh, what raggedy paper. We'll need lots of pictures to cover all the holes and spots."

"We'd better clean it all first," advised sensible Jean. "The windows are covered with dust and the floor is just black."

"This," said Marjory, opening a door, "must be the dining-room. Oh! What a cunning little corner cupboard—just the place for our dishes."

"You mean it would be if we had any," said Mabel. "Mine are all smashed."

"Pooh!" said Jean. "We don't mean doll things—we want real, grown-up ones. Why, what a cunning little bedroom!"

"There's one off the parlor, too," said Marjory, "and it's even cunninger than this."

"My! what a horrid place!" exclaimed Mabel, poking an inquisitive nose into another unexplored room, and as hastily withdrawing that offended feature. "Mercy, I'm all over spider webs."

"That's the kitchen," explained Bettie. "Most of the plaster has fallen down and it's rained in a good deal. But here's a good stovepipe hole, and such a cunning cupboard built into the wall. What have you found, Jean?"

"Just a pantry," said Jean, holding up a pair of black hands, "and lots of dust. There isn't a clean spot in the house."

"So much the better," said Bettie, whose clouds always had a silver lining. "We'll have just that much more fun cleaning up. I'll tell you what let's do—and we've all day tomorrow to do it in. We'll just regularly clean house—I've always wanted to clean house."

"Me too," cried Mabel, enthusiastically. "We'll bring just oceans of water—"

"There's water here," interrupted Jean, turning a faucet. "Water and a pretty good sink. The water runs out all right."

"That's good," said Bettie. "We must each bring a broom, and soap—"

"And rags," suggested Jean.

"And papers for the shelves," added Marjory.

"And wear our oldest clothes," said Bettie.

"Oo-ow, wow!" squealed Mabel.

"What's the matter?" asked the girls, rushing into the pantry.

"Spiders and mice," said Mabel. "I just poked my head into the cupboard and a mouse jumped out. I'm all spider-webby again, too."

"Well, there won't be any spiders by tomorrow night," said Bettie, consolingly, "or any mice either, if somebody will bring a cat. Now let's go home to supper—I'm hungry as a bear."

"Everybody remember to wear her oldest clothes," admonished Jean, "and to bring a broom."

"I'll tie the key to a string and wear it around my neck night and day," said Bettie, locking the door carefully when the girls were outside. "Aren't we going to have a perfectly glorious summer?"

When Mr. Black, on the way to his office the next morning, met his four little friends, he did not recognize them. Jean, who was fourteen, and tall for her age, wore one of her mother's calico wrappers tied in at the waist by the strings of the cook's biggest apron. Marjory, in the much shrunken gown of a previous summer, had her golden curls tucked away under the housemaid's sweeping cap. Bettie appeared in her very oldest skirt surmounted by an exceedingly ragged jacket and cap discarded by one of her brothers; while Mabel, with her usual enthusiasm, looked like a veritable rag-bag. When Bettie had unlocked the door—she had slept all night with the key in her hand to make certain that it would not escape—the girls filed in.

"I know how to handle a broom as well as anybody," said Mabel, giving a mighty sweep and raising such a cloud of dust that the four housecleaners were obliged to flee out of doors to keep from strangling.

"Phew!" said Jean, when she had stopped coughing. "I guess we'll have to take it out with a shovel. The dust must be an inch thick."

"Wait," cried Marjory, darting off, "I'll get Aunty's sprinkling can; then the stuff won't fly so."

After that the sweeping certainly went better. Then came the dusting.

"It really looks very well," said Bettie, surveying the result with her head on one side and an air of housewifely wisdom that would have been more impressive if her nose hadn't been perfectly black with soot. "It certainly does look better, but I'm afraid you girls have most of the dust on your faces. I don't see how you managed to do it. Just look at Mabel."

"Just look at yourself!" retorted Mabel, indignantly. "You've got the dirtiest face I ever saw."

"Never mind," said Jean, gently. "I guess we're all about alike. I've wiped all the dust off the walls of this parlor. Now I'm going to wash the windows and the woodwork, and after that I'm going to scrub the floor."

"Do you know how to scrub?" asked Marjory.

"No, but I guess I can learn. There! Doesn't that pane look as if a really-truly housemaid had washed it?"

"Oh, Mabel! Do look out!" cried Marjory.

But the warning came too late. Mabel stepped on the slippery bar of soap and sat down hard in a pan of water, splashing it in every direction. For a moment Mabel looked decidedly cross, but when she got up and looked at the tin basin, she began to laugh.

"That's a funny way to empty a basin, isn't it?" she said. "There isn't a drop of water left in it."

"Well, don't try it again," said Jean. "That's Mrs. Tucker's basin and you've smashed it flat. You should learn to sit down less suddenly."

"And," said Marjory, "to be more careful in your choice of seats— we'll have to take up a collection and buy Mrs. Tucker a new basin, or she'll be afraid to lend us anything more."

The girls ran home at noon for a hasty luncheon. Rested and refreshed, they all returned promptly to their housecleaning.

Nobody wanted to brush out the kitchen cupboard. It was not only dusty, but full of spider webs, and worst of all, the spiders themselves seemed very much at home. The girls left the back door open, hoping that the spiders would run out of their own accord. Apparently, however, the spiders felt no need of fresh air. Bettie, without a word to anyone, ran home, returning a moment later with her brother Bob's old tame crow blinking solemnly from her shoulder. She placed the great, black bird on the cupboard shelf and in a very few moments every spider had vanished down his greedy throat.

"He just loves them," said Bettie.

"How funny!" said Mabel. "Who ever heard of getting a crow to help clean house? I wish he could scrub floors as well as he clears out cupboards."

The scrubbing, indeed, looked anything but an inviting task. Jean succeeded fairly well with the parlor floor, though she declared when that was finished that her wrists were so tired that she couldn't hold the scrubbing-brush another moment. Marjory and Bettie together scrubbed the floor of the tiny dining-room. Mabel made a brilliant success of one of the little bedrooms, but only, the other girls said, by accidentally tipping over a pail of clean water upon it, thereby rinsing off a thick layer of soap. Then Jean, having rested for a little while, finished the remaining bedroom and Marjory scoured the pantry shelves.

The kitchen floor was rough and very dirty. Nobody wanted the task of scrubbing it. The tired girls leaned against the wall and looked at the floor and then at one another.

"Let's leave it until Monday," said Mabel, who looked very much as if the others had scrubbed the floor with her. "I've had all the house-cleaning I want for one day."

"Oh, no," pleaded Bettie. "Everything else is done. Just think how lovely it would be to go home tonight with all the disagreeable part finished! We could begin to move in Monday if we only had the house all clean."

"Couldn't we cover the dirtiest places with pieces of old carpet?" demanded Mabel.

"Oh, what dreadful housekeeping that would be!" said Marjory.

"Yes," said Jean, "we must have every bit of it nice. Perhaps if we sit on the doorstep and rest for a few moments we'll feel more like scrubbing."

The tired girls sat in a row on the edge of the low porch. They were all rather glad that the next day would be Sunday, for between the dandelions and the dust they had had a very busy week.

"Why!" said Bettie, suddenly brightening. "We're going to have a visitor, I do believe."

"Hi there!" said Mr. Black, turning in at the gate. "I smell soap. Housecleaning all done?"

"All," said Bettie, wearily, "except the kitchen floor, and, oh! we're so tired. I'm afraid we'll have to leave it until Monday, but we just hate to."

"Too tired to eat peanuts?" asked Mr. Black, handing Bettie a huge paper bag. "Stay right here on the doorstep, all of you, and eat every one of these nuts. I'll look around and see what you've been doing—I'm sure there can't be much dirt left inside when there's so much on your faces."

It seemed a pity that Mr. Black, who liked little girls so well, should have no children of his own. A great many years before Bettie's people had moved to Lakeville, he had had one sister; and at another almost equally remote period he had possessed one little daughter, a slender, narrow-chested little maid, with great, pathetic brown eyes, so like Bettie's that Mr. Black was startled when Dr. Tucker's little daughter had first smiled at him from the Tucker doorway, for the senior warden's little girl had lived to be only six years old. This, of course, was the secret of Mr. Black's affection for Bettie.

Mr. Black, who was a moderately stout, gray-haired man of fifty-five, with kind, dark eyes and a strong, rugged, smooth-shaven countenance, had a great deal of money, a beautiful home perched on the brow of a green hill overlooking the lake, and a silk hat. This last made a great impression on the children, for silk hats were seldom worn in Lakeville. Mr. Black looked very nice indeed in his, when he wore it to church Sunday morning, but Bettie felt more at home with him when he sat bareheaded on the rectory porch, with his short, crisp, thick gray hair tossed by the south wind.

Besides these possessions, Mr. Black owned a garden on the sheltered hillside where wonderful roses grew as they would grow nowhere else in Lakeville. This was fortunate because Mr. Black loved roses, and spent much time poking about among them with trowel and pruning shears. Then, there were shelves upon shelves of books in the big, dingy library, which was the one room that the owner of the large house really lived in. A public-spirited man, Mr. Black had a wide circle of acquaintances and a few warm friends; but with all his possessions, and in spite of a jovial, cheerful manner in company, his dark, rather stern face, as Bettie had very quickly discovered, was sad when he sat alone in his pew in church. He had really nothing in the world to love but his books and his roses. It was evident, to anyone who had time to think about it, that kind Mr. Black, whose wife had died so many years before that only the oldest townspeople could remember that he had had a wife, was, in spite of his comfortable circumstances, a very lonely man, and that, as he grew older, he felt his loneliness more keenly. There were others besides Bettie who realized this, but it was not an easy matter to offer sympathy to Mr. Black—there was a dignity about him that repelled anything that looked like pity. Bettie was the one person who succeeded, without giving offense, in doing this difficult thing, but Bettie did it unconsciously, without in the least knowing that she had accomplished it, and this, of course, was another reason for the strong friendship between Mr. Black and her.

The girls found the peanuts decidedly refreshing; their unusual exercise had given them astonishing appetites.

"I wonder," said Bettie, some ten minutes later, when the paper bag was almost empty, "what Mr. Black is doing in there."

"I think, from the swishing, swushing sounds I hear," said Jean, "that Mr. Black must be scrubbing the kitchen."

"What!" gasped the girls.

"Come and see," said Jean, stealing in on tiptoe.

There, sure enough, was stout Mr. Black dipping a broom every now and then into a pail of soapy water and vigorously sweeping the floor with it.

"I think," whispered Mabel, ruefully, "that that's Mother's best broom."

"Never mind," consoled Jean. "You can take mine home if you think she'll care. It's really mine because I bought it when we had that broom drill in the sixth grade. It's been hanging on my wall ever since."

"Hi there!" exclaimed Mr. Black, who, looking up suddenly, had discovered the smiling girls in the doorway. "You didn't know I could scrub, did you?"

Mr. Black, quite regardless of his spotless cuffs and his polished shoes, drew a bucket of fresh water and dashed it over the floor, sweeping the flood out of doors and down the back steps.

"There," said Mr. Black, standing the broom in the corner, "if there's a cleaner house in town than this, I don't know where you'll find it. In return for scrubbing this kitchen, of course, I shall expect you to invite me to dinner when you get to housekeeping."

"We will! We do!" shouted the girls. "And we'll cook every single thing ourselves."

"I don't know that I'll insist on that," returned Mr. Black, teasingly, "but I shan't let you forget about the dinner."

CHAPTER 4.
FURNISHING THE
COTTAGE

After tea that Saturday night four tired but spotlessly clean little girls sat on Jean's doorstep, making plans for the coming week.

"What are you going to do for a stove?" asked Mrs. Mapes.

"I have a toy one," replied Mabel, "but it has only one leg and it always smokes. Besides, I can't find it."

"I have a little box stove that the boys used to have in their camp," said Mrs. Mapes. "It has three good legs and it doesn't smoke at all. If you want it, and if you'll promise to be very careful about your fire, I'll have one of the boys set it up for you."

"That would be lovely," said Bettie, gratefully. "Mamma has given me four saucers and a syrup jug, and I have a few pieces left of quite a large-sized doll's tea set."

"We have an old rug," said Marjory, "that I'm almost sure I can have for the parlor floor, and I have two small rocking chairs of my own."

"There's a lot of old things in our garret," said Mabel; "three-legged tables, and chairs with the seats worn out. I know Mother'll let us take them."

"Well," said Bettie, "take everything you have to the cottage Monday afternoon after school. Bring all the pictures you can to cover the walls, and—"

"Hark!" said Mrs. Mapes. "I think somebody is calling Bettie."

"Oh, my!" said Bettie, springing to her feet. "This is bath night and I promised to bathe the twins. I must go this minute."

"I think Bettie is sweet," said Jean. "Mr. Black would never have given us the cottage if he hadn't been so fond of Bettie; but she doesn't put on any airs at all. She makes us feel as if it belonged to all of us."

"Bettie is a sweet little girl," said Mrs. Mapes, "but she's far too energetic for such a little body. You mustn't let her do all the work."

"Oh, we don't!" exclaimed Mabel, grandly. "Why, what are you laughing at, Marjory?"

"Oh, nothing," said Marjory. "I just happened to remember how you scrubbed that bedroom floor."

From four to six on Monday afternoon, the little housekeepers, heavily burdened each time with their goods and chattels, made many small journeys between their homes and Dandelion Cottage. The parlor was soon piled high with furniture that was all more or less battered.

"Dear me," said Jean, pausing at the door with an armful of carpet. "How am I ever to get in? Hadn't we better straighten out what we have before we bring anything more?"

"Yes," said Bettie. "I wouldn't be surprised if we had almost enough for two houses. I'm sure I've seen six clocks."

"That's only one for each room," said Mabel. "Besides, none of the four that I brought will go."

"Neither will my two," said Marjory, giggling.

"We might call this 'The House of the Tickless Clocks,'" suggested Jean.

"Or of the grindless coffee-mill," giggled Marjory.

"Or of the talkless telephone," added Mabel. "I brought over an old telephone box so we could pretend we had a telephone."

There were still several things lacking when the children had found places for all their crippled belongings. They had no couch for the sofa pillows Mabel had brought, but Bettie converted two wooden boxes and a long board into an admirable cozy corner. She even upholstered this sadly misnamed piece of furniture with the burlaps and excelsior that had been packed about her father's new desk, but it still needed a cover. The windows lacked curtains, the girls had only one fork, and their cupboard was so distressingly empty that it rivaled Mother Hubbard's.

They had planned to eat and even sleep at the cottage during vacation, which was still some weeks distant; but, as they had no beds and no provisions, and as their parents said quite emphatically that they could not stay away from home at night, part of this plan had to be given up.

Most of the grown-ups, however, were greatly pleased with the cottage plan. Marjory's Aunty Jane, who was nervous and disliked having children running in and out of her spotlessly neat house, was glad to have Marjory happy with her little friends, provided they were all perfectly safe—and out of earshot. Overworked Mrs. Tucker found it a great relief to have careful Bettie take two or three of the smallest children entirely off her hands for several hours each day. When these infants, divided as equally as possible among the four girls, were not needed indoors to serve as playthings, they rolled about contentedly inside the cottage fence. Mabel's mother did not hesitate to say that she, for one, was thankful enough that Mr. Black had given the girls a place to play in. With Mabel engaged elsewhere, it was possible, Mrs. Bennett said, to keep her own house quite respectably neat. Mrs. Mapes, indeed, missed quiet, orderly Jean; but she would not mention it for fear of spoiling her tender-hearted little daughter's pleasure, and it did not occur to modest Jean that she was of sufficient consequence to be missed by her mother or anyone else.

The neighbors, finding that the long-deserted cottage was again occupied, began to be curious about the occupants. One day Mrs. Bartholomew Crane, who lived almost directly opposite the cottage, found herself so devoured by kindly curiosity that she could stand it no longer. Intending to be neighborly, for Mrs. Crane was always neighborly in the best sense of the word, she put on her one good dress and started across the street to call on the newcomers.

It was really a great undertaking for Mrs. Crane to pay visits, for she was a stout, slow-moving person, and, owing to the antiquity and consequent tenderness of her best garments, it was an even greater undertaking for the good woman to make a visiting costume. Her best black silk, for instance, had to be neatly mended with court-plaster when all other remedies had failed, and her old, thread-lace collars had been darned until their original floral patterns had given place to a mosaic of spider webs. Mrs. Crane's motives, however, were far better than her clothes. Years before, when she was newly married, she had lived for months a stranger in a strange town, where it was no unusual occurrence to live for years in ignorance of one's next-door neighbor's very name. During those unhappy months poor Mrs. Crane, sociable by nature yet sadly afflicted with shyness, had suffered keenly from loneliness and homesickness. She had vowed then that no other stranger should suffer as she had suffered, if it were in her power to prevent it; so, in spite of increasing difficulties, kind Mrs. Crane conscientiously called on each newcomer. In many cases, hers was the first welcome to be extended to persons settling in Lakeville, and although these visits were prompted by single-minded generosity, it was natural that she should, at the same time, make many friends. These, however, were seldom lasting ones, for many persons, whose business kept them in Lakeville for perhaps only a few months, afterwards moved away and drifted quietly out of Mrs. Crane's life.

That afternoon the four girls realized for the first time that Dandelion Cottage was provided with a doorbell. In response to its lively jingling, Mabel dropped the potato she was peeling with neatness but hardly with dispatch, and hurried to the door.

"Is your moth—Is the lady of the house at home?" asked Mrs. Crane.

"Yes'm, all of us are—there's four," stammered Mabel, who wasn't quite sure of her ability to entertain a grown-up caller. "Please walk in. Oh! don't sit down in that one, please! There's only two legs on that chair, and it always goes down flat."

"Dear me," said Mrs. Crane, moving toward the cozy corner, "I shouldn't have suspected it."

"Oh, you can't sit there, either," exclaimed Mabel. "You see, that's the Tucker baby taking his nap."

"My land!" said stout Mrs. Crane. "I thought it was one of those new-fashioned roll pillows."

"This chair," said Mabel, dragging one in from the dining room, "is the safest one we have in the house, but you must be careful to sit right down square in the middle of it because it slides out from under you if you sit too hard on the front edge. If you'll excuse me just a minute I'll go call the others—they're making a vegetable garden in the back yard."

"Well, I declare!" said Mrs. Crane, when she had recognized the four young housekeepers and had heard all about the housekeeping. "It seems as if I ought to be able to find something in the way of furniture for you. I have a single iron bedstead I'm willing to lend you, and maybe I can find you some other things."

"Thank you very much," said Bettie, politely.

"I hope," said Mrs. Crane, pleasantly, "that you'll be very neighborly and come over to see me whenever you feel like it, for I'm always alone."

"Thank you," said Jean, speaking for the household. "We'd just love to."

"Haven't you any children?" asked Bettie, sympathetically.

"Not one," replied Mrs. Crane. "I've never had any but I've always loved children."

"But I'm sure you have a lot of grandchildren," said Mabel, consolingly. "You look so nice and grandmothery."

"No," said Mrs. Crane, not appearing so sorrowful as Mabel had supposed an utterly grandchildless person would look, "I've never possessed any grandchildren either."

"But," queried Mabel, who was sometimes almost too inquisitive, "haven't you any relatives, husbands, or anybody, in all the world?"

Many months afterward the girls were suddenly reminded of Mrs. Crane's odd, contradictory reply:

"No—Yes—that is, no. None to speak of, I mean. Do you girls sleep here, too?"

"No" said Jean. "We want to, awfully, but our mothers won't let us. You see, we sleep so soundly that they're all afraid we might get the house afire, burn up, and never know a thing about it."

"They're quite right," said Mrs. Crane. "I suppose they like to have you at home once in a while."

"Oh, they do have us," replied Bettie. "We eat and sleep at home and they have us all day Sundays. When they want any of us other times, all they have to do is to open a back window and call—Dear me, Mrs. Crane, I'll have to ask you to excuse me this very minute—There's somebody calling me now."

Other visitors, including the girls' parents, called at the cottage and seemed to enjoy it very much indeed. The visitors were always greatly interested and everybody wanted to help. One brought a little table that really stood up very well if kept against the wall, another found curtains for all the windows—a little ragged, to be sure, but still curtains. Grandma Pike, who had a wonderful garden, was so delighted with everything that she gave the girls a crimson petunia growing in a red tomato can, and a great many neat little homemade packets of flower seeds. Rob said they might have even his porcupine if they could get it out from under the rectory porch.

By the end of the week the cottage presented quite a lived-in appearance. Bright pictures covered the dingy paper, and, thanks to numerous donations, the rooms looked very well furnished. No one would have suspected that the chairs were untrustworthy, the tables crippled, and the clocks devoid of works. The cottage seemed cozy and pleasant, and the girls kept it in apple-pie order.

Out of doors, the grass was beginning to show and little green specks dotted the flower beds. Other green specks in crooked rows staggered across the vegetable garden.

The four mothers, satisfied that their little daughters were safe in Dandelion Cottage, left them in undisturbed possession.

"I declare," said Mrs. Mapes one day, "the only time I see Jean, nowadays, is when she's asleep. All the rest of the time she's in school or at the cottage."

"Yes," said Mrs. Bennett, "when I miss my scissors or any of my dishes or anything else, I always have to go to the cottage and get out a search warrant. Mabel has carried off a wagonload of things, but I don't know when our own house has been so peaceful."

CHAPTER 5.
POVERTY IN THE COTTAGE

"There's no use talking," said Jean, one day, as the girls sat at their dining-room table eating very smoky toast and drinking the weakest of cocoa, "we'll have to get some provisions of our own before long if we're going to invite Mr. Black to dinner as we promised. The cupboard's perfectly empty and Bridget says I can't take another scrap of bread or one more potato out of the house this week."

"Aunty Jane says there'll be trouble," said Marjory, "if I don't keep out of her ice box, so I guess I can't bring any more milk. When she says there'll be trouble, there usually is, if I'm not pretty careful. But dear me, it is such fun to cook our own meals on that dear little box-stove, even if most of the things do taste pretty awful."

"I wish," said Mabel, mournfully, "that somebody would give us a hen, so we could make omelets."

"Who ever made omelets out of a hen?" asked Jean, laughing.

"I meant out of the eggs, of course," said Mabel, with dignity. "Hens lay eggs, don't they? If we count on five or six eggs a day—"

"The goose that laid the golden egg laid only one a day," said Marjory. "It seems to me that six is a good many."

"I wasn't talking about geese," said Mabel, "but about just plain everyday hens."

"Six-every-day hens, you mean, don't you?" asked Marjory, teasingly. "You'd better wish for a cow, too, while you're about it."

"Yes," said Bettie, "we certainly need one, for I'm not to ask for butter more than twice a week. Mother says she'll be in the poorhouse before summer's over if she has to provide butter for two families."

"I just tell you what it is, girls," said Jean, nibbling her cindery crust, "we'll just have to earn some money if we're to give Mr. Black any kind of a dinner."

Mabel, who always accepted new ideas with enthusiasm, slipped quietly into the kitchen, took a solitary lemon from the cupboard, cut it in half, and squeezed the juice into a broken-nosed pitcher. This done, she added a little sugar and a great deal of water to the lemon juice, slipped quietly out of the back door, ran around the house and in at the front door, taking a small table from the front room. This she carried out of doors to the corner of the lot facing the street, where she established her lemonade stand.

She was almost immediately successful, for the day was warm, and Mrs. Bartholomew Crane, who was entertaining two visitors on her front porch, was glad of an opportunity to offer her guests something in the way of refreshment. The cottage boasted only one glass that did not leak, but Mabel cheerfully made three trips across the street with it—it did not occur to any of them until too late it would have been easier to carry the pitcher across in the first place. The lemonade was decidedly weak, but the visitors were too polite to say so. On her return, a thirsty small boy offered Mabel a nickel for all that was left in the pitcher, and Mabel, after a moment's hesitation, accepted the offer.

"You're getting a bargain," said Mabel. "There's as much as a glass and three quarters there, besides all the lemon."

"Did you get a whole pitcherful out of one lemon?" asked the boy. "You'd be able to make circus lemonade all right."

Before the other girls had had time to discover what had become of her, the proprietor of the lemonade stand marched into the cottage and proudly displayed four shining nickels and the empty pitcher.

"Why, where in the world did you get all that?" cried Marjory. "Surely you never earned it by being on time for meals—you've been late three times a day ever since we got the cottage."

"Sold lemonade," said Mabel. "Our troubles are over, girls. I'm going to buy two lemons tomorrow and sell twice as much."

"Good!" cried Bettie, "I'll help. The boys have promised to bring me a lot of arbutus tonight—they went to the woods this morning. I'll tie it in bunches and perhaps we can sell that, too."

"Wouldn't it be splendid if we could have Mr. Black here to dinner next Saturday?" said Jean. "I'll never be satisfied until we've kept that promise, but I don't suppose we could possibly get enough things together by that time."

"I have a sample can of baking powder," offered Marjory, hopefully. "I'll bring it over next time I come."

"What's the good?" asked matter-of-fact Mabel. "We can't feed Mr. Black on just plain baking powder, and we haven't any biscuits to raise with it."

"Dear me," said Jean, "I wish we hadn't been so extravagant at first. If we hadn't had so many tea parties last week, we might get enough flour and things at home. Mother says it's too expensive having all her groceries carried off."

"Never mind," consoled Mabel, confidently. "We'll be buying our own groceries by this time tomorrow with the money we make selling lemonade. A boy said my lemonade was quite as good as you can buy at the circus."

Unfortunately, however, it rained the next day and the next, so lemonade was out of the question. By the time it cleared, Bettie's neat little bunches of arbutus were no longer fresh, and careless Mabel had forgotten where she had put the money. She mentioned no fewer than twenty-two places where the four precious nickels might be, but none of them happened to be the right one.

"Mercy me," said Bettie, "it's dreadful to be so poor! I'm afraid we'll have to invite Mr. Black to one of our bread-and-sugar tea-parties, after all."

"No," said Jean, firmly. "We've just got to give him a regular seven-course dinner—he has 'em every day at home. We'll have to put it off until we can do it in style."

"By and by," said Mabel, "we'll have beans and radishes and things in our own garden, and we can go to the woods for berries."

"Perhaps," said Bettie, hopefully, "one of the boys might catch a fish—Rob almost did, once."

"I suppose I could ask Aunty Jane for a potato once in a while," said Marjory, "but I'll have to give her time to forget about last month's grocery bill—she says we never before used so many eggs in one month and I guess Maggie did give me a good many. Potatoes will keep, you know. We can save 'em until we have enough for a meal."

"While we're about it," said Bettie, "I think we'd better have Mrs. Crane to dinner, too. She's such a nice old lady and she's been awfully good to us."

"She's not very well off," agreed Mabel, "and probably a real, first-class dinner would taste good to her."

"But," pleaded Bettie, "don't let's ask her until we're sure of the date. As it is, I can't sleep nights for thinking of how Mr. Black must feel. He'll think we don't want him."

"You'd better explain to him," suggested Jean, "that it isn't convenient to have him just yet, but that we're going to just as soon as ever we can. We mustn't tell him why, because it would be just like him to send the provisions here himself, and then it wouldn't really be our party."

In spite of all the girls' plans, however, by the end of the week the cottage larder was still distressingly empty. Marjory had, indeed, industriously collected potatoes, only to have them carried off by an equally industrious rat; and Mabel's four nickels still remained missing. Things in the vegetable garden seemed singularly backward, possibly because the four eager gardeners kept digging them up to see if they were growing. Their parents and Marjory's Aunty Jane were firmer than ever in their refusal to part with any more staple groceries.

Perhaps if the girls had explained why they wanted the things, their relatives would have been more generous; but girllike, the four poverty-stricken young housekeepers made a deep mystery of their dinner plan. It was their most cherished secret, and when they met each morning they always said, mysteriously, "Good morning—remember M. B. D.," which meant, of course, "Mr. Black's Dinner."

Mr. Black, indeed, never went by without referring to the girls' promise.

"When," he would ask, "is that dinner party coming off? It's a long time since I've been invited to a first-class dinner, cooked by four accomplished young ladies, and I'm getting hungrier every minute. When I get up in the morning I always say: 'Now I won't eat much breakfast because I've got to save room for that dinner'—and then, after all, I don't get invited."

The situation was growing really embarrassing. The girls began to feel that keeping house, not to mention giving dinner parties, with no income whatever, was anything but a joke.

CHAPTER 6.
A LODGER TO THE RESCUE

G rass was beginning to grow on the tiny lawn, all sorts of thrifty young seedlings were popping up in the flower beds, and Jean's pansies were actually beginning to blossom. The girls had trained the rampant Virginia creeper away from the windows and had coaxed it to climb the porch pillars. From the outside, no one would have suspected that Dandelion Cottage was not occupied by a regular grown-up family. Book agents and peddlers offered their wares at the front door, and appeared very much crestfallen when Bettie, or one of the others, explained that the neatly kept little cottage was just a playhouse. Handbills and sample packages of yeast cakes were left on the doorstep, and once a brand-new postman actually dropped a letter into the letter-box; Mabel carried it afterward to Mrs. Bartholomew Crane, to whom it rightfully belonged.

One afternoon, when Jean was rearranging the dining-room pictures—they had to be rearranged very frequently—and when Mabel and Marjory were busy putting fresh papers on the pantry shelves,

A middle-aged young lady stood on the door-step.

there was a ring at the doorbell.

Bettie, who had been dusting the parlor, pushed the chairs into place, threw her duster into the dining-room and ran to the door. A lady—Bettie described her afterwards as a "middle-aged young lady with the sweetest dimple"—stood on the doorstep.

"Is your mother at home?" asked the lady, smiling pleasantly at Bettie, who liked the stranger at once.

"She—she doesn't live here," said Bettie, taken by surprise.

"Perhaps you can tell me what I want to know. I'm a stranger in town and I want to rent a room in this neighborhood. I am to have my meals at Mrs. Baker's, but she hasn't any place for me to sleep. I don't want anything very expensive, but of course I'd be willing to pay a fair price. Do you know of anybody with rooms to rent? I'm to be in town for three weeks."

Bettie shook her head, reflectively. "No, I don't believe I do, unless—"

Bettie paused to look inquiringly at Jean, who, framed by the dining-room doorway, was nodding her head vigorously.

"Perhaps Jean does," finished Bettie.

"Are you very particular," asked Jean, coming forward, "about what kind of room it is?"

"Why, not so very," returned the guest. "I'm afraid I couldn't afford a very grand one."

"Are you very timid?" asked Bettie, who had suddenly guessed what Jean had in mind. "I mean are you afraid of burglars and mice and things like that?"

"Why, most persons are, I imagine," said the young woman, whose eyes were twinkling pleasantly. "Are there a great many mice and burglars in this neighborhood?"

"Mice," said Jean, "but not burglars. It's a very honest neighborhood. I think I have an idea, but you see there are four of us and I'll have to consult the others about it, too. Sit here, please, in the cozy corner—it's the safest piece of furniture we have. Now if you'll excuse us just a minute we'll go to the kitchen and talk it over."

"Certainly," murmured the lady, who looked a trifle embarrassed at encountering the gaze of the forty-two staring dolls that sat all around the parlor with their backs against the baseboard. "I hope I haven't interrupted a party."

"Not at all," assured Bettie, with her best company manner.

"Girls," said Jean, when she and Bettie were in the kitchen with the door carefully closed behind them, "would you be willing to rent the front bedroom to a clean, nice-looking lady if she'd be willing to take it? She wants to pay for a room, she says, and she looks very polite and pleasant, doesn't she, Bettie?"

"Yes," corroborated Bettie, "I like her. She has kind of twinkling brown eyes and such nice dimples."

"You see," explained Jean, "the money would pay for Mr. Black's dinner."

"Why, so it would," cried Marjory. "Let's do it."

"Yes," echoed Mabel, "for goodness' sake, let's do it. It's only three weeks, anyway, and what's three weeks!"

"How would it be," asked Marjory, cautiously, "to take her on approval? Aunty Jane always has hats and things sent on approval, so she can send them back if they don't fit."

"Splendid!" cried Mabel. "If she doesn't fit Dandelion Cottage, she can't stay."

"Oh," gurgled Marjory, "what a dinner we'll give Mr. Black and Mrs. Crane! We'll have ice cream and—"

"Huh!" said Mabel, "most likely she won't take the room at all. Anyhow, probably she's got tired of waiting and has gone."

"We'll go and see," said Jean. "Come on, everybody."

The lady, however, still sat on the hard, lumpy cozy corner, with her toes just touching the ground.

"Well," said she, smiling at the flock of girls, "how about the idea?"

The other three looked expectantly at Jean; Mabel nudged her elbow and Bettie nodded at her.

"You talk," said Marjory; "you're the oldest."

"It's like this," explained Jean. "This house isn't good enough to rent to grown-ups because it's all out of repair, so they've lent it to us for the summer for a playhouse. The back of it leaks dreadfully when it rains, and the plaster is all down in the kitchen, but the front bedroom is really very nice—if you don't mind having four kinds of carpet on the floor. This is a very safe neighborhood, no tramps or anything like that, and if you're not an awfully timid person, perhaps you wouldn't mind staying alone at night."

"If you did," added Bettie, "probably one of us could sleep in the other room unless it happened to rain—it rains right down on the bed."

"Could I go upstairs to look at the room?" asked the young woman.

"There isn't any upstairs," said Bettie, pulling back a curtain; "the room's right here."

"Why! What a dear little room—all white and blue!"

"I hope you don't mind having children around," said Marjory, somewhat anxiously. "You see, we'd have to play in the rest of the house."

"Of course," added Jean, hastily, "if you had company you could use the parlor—"

"And the front steps," said Bettie.

"I'm very fond of children," said the young lady, "and I don't expect to have any company but you because I don't know anybody here. I shall be away every day until about five o'clock because I am here with my father who is tuning church organs, and I have to help him. I strike the notes while he works behind the organ. He has a room at Mrs. Baker's, but she didn't have any place to put me. I think I should like this little room very much indeed. Now, how much are you going to charge me for it?"

Jean looked at Bettie, and Bettie looked at the other two.

"I don't know," said Jean, at last.

"Neither do I," said Bettie.

"Would—would a dollar a week be too much?" asked Marjory.

"It wouldn't be enough," said the young woman, promptly. "My father pays five for the room he has, but it's really a larger room than he wanted. I should be very glad to give you two dollars and a half a week—I'm sure I couldn't find a furnished room anywhere for less than that. Can I move in tonight? I've nothing but a small trunk."

"Ye-es," said Bettie, looking inquiringly at Jean. "I think we could get it ready by seven o'clock. It's all perfectly clean, but you see we'll have to change things around a little and fix up the washstand."

"I'm sure," said the visitor, turning to depart, "that it all looks quite lovely just as it is. You may expect me at seven."

"Well," exclaimed Marjory, when the door had closed behind their pleasant visitor, "isn't this too grand for words! It's just like finding a bush with pennies growing on it, or a pot of gold at the end of the rainbow. Two and a half a week! That's—let me see. Why! that's seven dollars and a half! We can buy Mr. Black's dinner and have enough money left to live on for a long time afterwards."

"Mercy!" cried Mabel. "We never said a word to her about taking her on approval. We didn't even ask her name."

"Pshaw!" said Jean. "She's all right. She couldn't be disagreeable if she wanted to with that dimple and those sparkles in her eyes; but, girls, we've a tremendous lot to do."

"Yes," said Mabel. "If she'd known that the pillows under those ruffled shams were just flour sacks stuffed with excelsior, she wouldn't have thought everything so lovely. Girls, what in the world are we to do for sheets? We haven't even one."

"And blankets?" said Marjory.

"And quilts?" said Bettie. "That old white spread is every bit of bedclothes we own. I was so afraid she'd turn the cover down and see that everything else was just pieces of burlap."

"It's a good thing the mattress is all right," said Marjory. "But there isn't any bottom to the water pitcher, and the basin leaks like anything."

"We'll just have to go home," said Jean, "and tell our mothers all about it. We'll have to borrow what we need. We must get a lamp too, and some oil, because there isn't any other way of lighting the house."

The four girls ran first of all to Bettie's house with their surprising news.

"But, Bettie," said Mrs. Tucker, when her little daughter, helped by the other three, had explained the situation, "are you sure she's nice? I'm afraid you've been a little rash."

"Just as nice as can be," assured Bettie.

"Yes," said Dr. Tucker, "I guess it's all right. I know the organ tuner—I used to see him twice a year when we lived in Ohio. His name is Blossom and he's a very fine old fellow. I met his daughter this afternoon when they were examining the church organ, and she seemed a pleasant, well-educated young woman—I believe he said she teaches a kindergarten during the winter. The girls haven't made any mistake this time."

"Then we must make her comfortable," said Mrs. Tucker. "You may take sheets and pillow-cases from the linen closet, Bettie, and you must see that she has everything she needs."

Excited Bettie danced off to the linen closet and the others ran home to tell the good news.

"I've filled a lamp for you, Bettie," said Mrs. Tucker, meeting Bettie, with her arms full of sheets at the bottom of the stairs. "Here's a box of matches, too."

When Bettie was returning with her spoils to Dandelion Cottage she almost bumped into Mabel, whom she met at the gate with a pillow under each arm, a folded patchwork quilt balanced unsteadily on her head, and her chubby hands clasped about a big brass lamp.

"The pillows are off my own bed," said Mabel. "Mother wasn't home, but she wouldn't care, anyway."

"But can you sleep without them?"

"Oh, I'll take home one of the excelsior ones," said Mabel. "I can sleep on anything."

Jean came in a moment later with a pile of blankets and quilts. She, too, had a lamp, packed carefully in a big basket that hung from her arm. Marjory followed almost at her heels with more bedding, towels, a fourth lamp, and two candlesticks.

"Well," laughed Bettie, when all the lamps and candles were placed in a row on the dining-room table, "I guess Miss Blossom will have almost light enough. Here are four big lamps and two candles—"

"I've six more candles in my blouse," said Mabel, laughing and fishing them out one at a time. "I thought they'd do for the blue candlesticks Mrs. Crane gave us for the bedroom."

"Isn't it fortunate," said Jean, who was thumping the mattress vigorously, "that we put the best bed in this room? Beds are such hard things to move."

"Ye-es," said Bettie, rather doubtfully, "but I think we'd better tell Miss Blossom not to be surprised if the slats fall out once in a while during the night. You know they always do if you happen to turn over too suddenly."

"We must warn her about the chairs, too," said Marjory. "They're none of them really very safe."

"I guess," said Jean, "I'd better bring over the rocking chair from my own room, but I'm afraid she'll just have to grin and bear the slats, because they will fall out in spite of anything I can do."

By seven o'clock the room was invitingly comfortable. The washstand, which was really only a wooden box thinly disguised by a muslin curtain gathered across the front and sides, was supplied with a sound basin, a whole pitcher, numerous towels, and four kinds of soap—the girls had all thought of soap. They were unable to decide which kind the lodger would like best, so they laid Bettie's clear amber cake of glycerine soap, Jean's scentless white castile, Marjory's square of green cucumber soap, and Mabel's highly perfumed oval pink cake, in a rainbow row on the washstand.

The bed, bountifully supplied with coverings—had Dandelion Cottage been suddenly transported to Alaska the lodger would still have had blankets to spare, so generously had her enthusiastic landladies provided—looked very comfortable indeed. At half-past seven when the lodger arrived with apologies for being late because the drayman who was to move her trunk had been slow, the cottage, for the first time since the girls had occupied it, was brilliantly lighted.

"We thought," explained Bettie, "that you might feel less frightened in a strange place if you had plenty of light, though we didn't really mean to have so many lamps—we each supposed we were bringing the only one. Anyway, we don't know which one burns best."

"If they should all go out," said Mabel, earnestly, "there are candles and matches on the little shelf above the bed."

When the lodger had been warned about the loose slats and the untrustworthiness of the chairs, the girls said good-night.

"You needn't go on my account," said Miss Blossom. "It's pleasant to have you here—still, I'm not afraid to stay alone. You must always do just as you like about staying, you know; I shouldn't like to think that I was driving you out of this dear little house, for it was nice of you to let me come. I think I was very fortunate in finding a room so near Mrs. Baker's."

"Thank you," said Jean, "but we always have to be home before dark unless we have permission to stay any place."

"I have to go," confided Mabel, "because I was so excited that I forgot to eat my supper."

"So did I," said Marjory, frankly, "and I'm just as hungry as a bear."

"Everybody come home with me," said Jean. "We always have dinner later than you do and the things can't be very cold."

CHAPTER 7.
THE GIRLS DISCLOSE
A PLAN

"Did you sleep well, Miss Blossom?" asked Bettie, shyly waylaying the lodger who was on her way to breakfast.

"Ye-es," said Miss Blossom, smiling brightly, "though in spite of your warning and all my care, the bottom dropped out of my bed and landed the mattress on the floor. But no harm was done. As soon as I discovered that I was not falling down an elevator shaft, I went to sleep again. I think if I had a few nails and some little blocks of wood I could fix those slats so they'd stay in better; you see they're not quite long enough for the bed."

"I'll find some for you," said Bettie. "You'll find them on the parlor table when you get back."

Before the week was over, the girls had discovered that their new friend was in every way a most delightful person. She proved surprisingly skillful with hammer and nails, and besides mending the bed she soon had several of the chairs quite firm on their legs.

"Why," cried Bettie one day as she delightedly inspected an old black walnut rocker that had always collapsed at the slightest touch, "this old chair is almost strong enough to walk! I'm so glad you've made so many of them safe, because, when Mrs. Bartholomew Crane comes to see us, she's always afraid to sit down. She's such a nice neighbor that we'd like to make her comfortable."

"We do have the loveliest friends," said Jean, with a contented sigh. "It's hard to tell which is the nicest one."

"But the dearest two," exclaimed Marjory, discriminating nicely, "are Mr. Black and Mrs. Crane—except you, of course, Miss Blossom."

"Somehow," added Bettie, "we always think of those two in one breath, like Dombey and Son, or Jack and Jill."

"But they couldn't be farther apart really," declared Jean. "They're both nice, both are kind of old, both are dark and rather stout, but except for that they're altogether different. Mr. Black has everything in the world that anybody could want, and Mrs. Crane hasn't much of anything. Mr. Black is invited to banquets and things and rides in carriages and—"

"Has a silk hat," Mabel broke in.

"And Mrs. Crane," continued Jean, paying no attention to the interruption, "can't even afford to ride in the street car—I've heard her say so."

"I wish," groaned generous Mabel, with deep contrition, "that I'd never taken a cent for that lemonade I sold her last spring. If I'd dreamed how good and how poor she was, I wouldn't have. She might have had four rides with that money."

"I wish," said Jean, "we could do something perfectly grand and beautiful for Mrs. Crane. She's always doing the kindest little things for other people."

"Well," demanded Marjory, "aren't we going to have her here to dinner, too, when we have Mr. Black? Please don't tell anybody, Miss Blossom—it's to be a surprise."

"Still, just a dinner doesn't seem to be enough," said Jean, who, with her chin in her hand, seemed to be thinking deeply. "Of course it helps, but I'd rather save her life or do something like that."

"Little things count for a great deal in this world, sometimes," said Miss Blossom, leaning down to brush her cheek softly against Jean's. "It's generally wiser to leave the big things until one is big enough to handle them."

"Mrs. Crane is pretty big," offered matter-of-fact Mabel.

"Oh, dear," laughed Miss Blossom, "that wasn't at all what I meant."

"Mr. Black," said Bettie, dreamily, "has enough things, but I don't believe he really cares about anything in the world but his roses. His face is different when he talks about them, kind of soft all about the corners and not so—not so—"

"Daniel Webstery," supplied Jean, understandingly.

"It must be pretty lonely for him without any family," agreed Miss Blossom. "I don't know what would become of Father if he didn't have me to keep him cheered up—we're wonderful chums, Father and I."

"Oh", mourned tender-hearted Bettie, "I wish I could make Mrs. Crane rich enough so she wouldn't need to mend all the time, and that I could provide Mr. Black with some really truly relatives to love him the way you love your father."

"Oh, Bettie! Bettie!" cried Mabel, suddenly beginning, in her excitement, to bounce up and down on the one chair that possessed springs. "I know exactly how we could help them both. We could beg seven or eight children from the orphan asylum—they're glad to give 'em away—and let Mrs. Crane sell 'em to Mr. Black for—for ten dollars apiece."

Such a storm of merriment followed this simple solution of the problem that Mabel for the moment looked quite crushed. Her chair, incidentally, was crushed too, for Mabel's final bounce proved too much for its frail constitution; its four legs spread suddenly and lowered the surprised Mabel gently to the floor. Everybody laughed again, Mabel as heartily as anyone, and, for a time, the sorrows of Mrs. Crane and Mr. Black were forgotten.

The dinner party, however, still remained uppermost in all their plans. Mabel was in favor of giving it at once, but the other girls were more cautious, so the little mistresses of Dandelion Cottage finally decided to postpone the party until after Miss Blossom had paid her rent in full.

"You see," explained cautious Marjory, one day when the girls were alone, "she might get called away suddenly before the three weeks are up, and if we spent more money than we have it wouldn't be very comfortable. Besides, I've never seen seven dollars and a half all at once, and I'd like to."

But the dinner plan was no longer the profound secret that it had been at first, for when the young housekeepers had told their mothers about their lodger, they had been obliged to tell them also what they intended to do with the money. In the excitement of the moment, they had all neglected to mention Mrs. Crane, but later, when they made good this omission, their news was received in a most perplexing fashion. The girls were greatly puzzled, but they did not happen to compare notes until after something that happened at the dinner party had reminded them of their parents' incomprehensible behavior.

"Mamma," said Bettie, one evening at supper time, soon after Miss Blossom's arrival, "I forgot to tell you that we're going to ask Mrs. Crane, too, when we have Mr. Black to dinner. It's to be a surprise for both of them."

"What!" gasped Mrs. Tucker, dropping her muffin, and looking not at Bettie, but at Dr. Tucker. "Surely not Mrs. Crane and Mr. Black, too! You don't mean both at the same time!"

"Why, yes, Mamma," said Bettie. "It wouldn't cost any more."

Then the little girl looked with astonishment first at her father and then at her mother, for Dr. Tucker, with a warning finger against his lips, was shaking his head just as hard as he could at Mrs. Tucker, who looked the very picture of amazement.

"Why," asked Bettie, "what's the matter? Don't you think it's a good plan? Isn't it the right thing to do?"

"Yes," said Dr. Tucker, still looking at Bettie's mother, who was nodding her approval, "I shouldn't be surprised if it might prove a very good thing to do. Your idea of making it a surprise to both of them is a good one, too. I should keep it the darkest kind of secret until the very last moment, if I were you."

"Yes," agreed Mrs. Tucker, "I should certainly keep it a secret."

Jean, too, happened to mention the matter at home and with very much the same result. Mr. Mapes looked at Mrs. Mapes with something in his eye that very closely resembled an amused twinkle, and Jean was almost certain that there was an answering twinkle in her mother's eye.

"What's the joke?" asked Jean.

"I couldn't think of spoiling it by telling," said Mrs. Mapes. "If there's anything I can do to help you with your dinner party I shall be delighted to do it."

"Oh, will you?" cried Jean. "When I told you about it last week I thought, somehow, that you weren't very much interested."

"I'm very much interested indeed," returned Mrs. Mapes. "I hope you'll be able to keep the surprise part of it a secret to the very last moment. That's always the best part of a dinner party, you know."

"Yes," said Mr. Mapes, "if you know who the other guests are to be, it always takes away part of the pleasure."

When Marjory told the news, her Aunty Jane, who seldom smiled and who usually appeared to care very little about the doings in Dandelion Cottage, greatly surprised her niece by suddenly displaying as many as seven upper teeth; she showed, too, such flattering interest in the coming event that Marjory plucked up courage to ask for potatoes and other provisions that might prove useful.

"When you've decided what day you're going to have your party," said Aunty Jane, with astonishing good nature, "I'll give or lend you anything you want, provided you don't tell either of your guests who the other one is to be."

When Mabel told about the plan, she too was very much perplexed at the way her news was received. Her parents, after one speaking glance at each other, leaned back in their chairs and laughed until the tears rolled down their cheeks. But they, too, heartily approved of the dinner party and advised strict secrecy regarding the guests.

School was out, and, as Bettie said, every day was Saturday, but the days were slipping away altogether too rapidly. The lawn, by this time, was covered with what Mabel called "real grass," great bunches of Jean's sweetest purple pansies had to be picked every morning so they wouldn't go to seed, and the long bed by the fence threatened to burst at any moment into blossom. Even the much-disturbed vegetable garden was doing so nicely that it was possible to tell the lettuce from the radish plants.

Two of Miss Blossom's three weeks had gone. She herself was to leave town the following Thursday, and the dinner party was to take place the day after; but even the thought of the great event failed to keep the little cottagers quite cheerful, for they hated to think of losing their lovely lodger. Whenever this charming young person was not busy at one or another of the various churches with her father, she was playing with the children. "Just exactly," said Bettie, "as if she were just twelve years old, too." Her clever fingers made dresses for each of the four biggest dolls, and such cunning baby bonnets for each of the four littlest ones.

Best of all, she taught the girls how to do a great many things. She showed them how to turn the narrowest of hems, how to gather a ruffle neatly, and how to take the tiniest of stitches. Bettie, who had to help with the weekly darning, and Marjory, who had to mend her own stockings, actually found it pleasant work after Miss Blossom had shown them several different ways of weaving the threads.

"I just wish," cried Mabel, one day, in a burst of gratitude, "that you'd fall ill, or something so we could do something for you. You're just lovely to us."

"Thank you, Mabel," said Miss Blossom, with eyes that twinkled delightedly, "I'm sure you'd take beautiful care of me—I'm almost tempted to try it. Shall I have measles, or just plain smallpox?"

CHAPTER 8.
AN UNEXPECTED CROP
OF DANDELIONS

In spite of the prospect of losing her, the last week of Miss Blossom's stay was a delightful one to the girls because so many pleasant things happened. The best of all concerned the cottage dining-room.

This room had proved the hardest spot in the house to make attractive, for it seemed to resist all efforts to make a well-furnished room of it. Most of the faded paper was loose and much of it had dropped off in patches during the time that the cottage was vacant, showing the ugly, dark, painted wall underneath. It was only too evident that the pictures that the girls had fastened up carefully with pins had been put up for purposes of concealment, the ceiling was stained and dingy, and the rug was far too small to cover the floor where some industrious former occupant had daubed paint of various gaudy hues while trying, perhaps, to find the right shade for the woodwork.

Moreover, what little furniture there was in the dining-room showed very plainly that it had not been intended originally for dining-room use; the buffet, in particular, proclaimed loudly in big black letters that it was nothing but a soap box, and Bettie's best efforts could not make anything else of it. Now that the day for the long-postponed dinner party was actually set, the girls' attention was more than ever directed toward the forlorn appearance of the little dining-room.

"Dear me," said Bettie, one day when the five friends, seated around the table, were cutting out pictures for a wonderful scrap-book for the little lame boy whom Miss Blossom had discovered living near one of the churches, "I do wish this dining-room didn't look so sort of bedroomy."

"Yes," said Jean, "I've tried putting the buffet in every corner and all around the walls, and it won't look like anything but a wooden box."

"I tried covering it with a gathered curtain," said Mabel, "but that made it look so like a washstand that I took it off again."

"Why," exclaimed Miss Blossom, "you've given me a beautiful idea! I believe we could make a splendid sideboard out of that piano box that's so in our way on the back porch. We'd just have to saw the ends down a little, nail on some boards, paint it some plain, dark color, and spread a towel over the top, and we'd have a beautiful Flemish oak sideboard. I'll buy the can of paint."

"I'll do the painting," said Jean. "I helped Mother paint our kitchen floor, so I know a little about it."

"That would be lovely. I've been thinking, too, that it would be a good idea to fix a little shelf under this window to hold your petunia and these two geraniums that are suffering so for sunshine. I think I could make it from the boards in that soap box."

"Oh, thank you!" cried Bettie. "I don't believe there's anything you don't know how to do."

The piano box, transformed by Miss Blossom and the four girls into a very good imitation of a Flemish oak sideboard, did indeed make such an imposing piece of furniture that the rest of the room looked shabbier than ever by contrast.

"I'm afraid," said Miss Blossom, surveying the effect with an air of comical dismay, "that the rest of our dining-room really looks worse than it did before; it's like trying to wear a new hat with an old gown. But I'm proud of our handiwork."

"Yes," said Jean, "it's a great deal more like a sideboard than it is like a piano box."

"It's the sideboardiest sideboard I ever saw," said Mabel, "but it's certainly too fine for this room."

"Never mind," said cheerful Bettie. "We'll let Mr. Black sit so he can see the sideboard, and we'll have Mrs. Crane face the geraniums on that cunning shelf. If their eyes begin to wander around the room we'll just call their attention to the things we want them to see. When Mamma entertains the sewing society she always invites the first one that comes to sit in the chair over the hole in the sitting-room rug so the others won't notice it. If we catch Mr. Black looking at the ceiling we'll say: 'Oh, Mr. Black, did you notice the flowers on the sideboard?'"

Everybody laughed at Bettie's comical idea. This desperate measure, however, was not needed, for one afternoon, the day after the sideboard was finished, something happened, something lovelier than the girls had ever even dreamed could happen.

It was only three o'clock, yet there was Miss Blossom coming home two whole hours earlier than usual; her white-haired father was with her and under his arm in a long parcel were seven rolls of wall paper.

"My contribution to the cottage," said Mr. Blossom, laying the bundle at Bettie's feet and smiling pleasantly at the row of girls on the doorstep.

"It's paper for the dining-room," explained Miss Blossom. "We happened to pass a store, on our way to work this noon, where they were advertising a sale of odd rolls of very nice paper at only five cents a roll. There were two rolls that were just right for the ceiling, and five rolls for the side wall. It seemed just exactly the right thing for Dandelion Cottage, so we couldn't help buying it."

"It would have been wicked," said Mr. Blossom, cutting the string about the bundle, "not to buy such suitable paper at such a ridiculous price."

"Oh! oh!" cried the delighted girls, as Mr. Blossom held up a roll for inspection. "It might have been made for this house!"

"Dandelion blossoms in yellow, with such lovely soft green leaves," said Bettie, "and such a lovely, light, creamy background. Oh! what's that?"

"That's the border," replied Miss Blossom. "See how graceful the pattern is, and how saucily those dandelions hold their heads. Show them the ceiling paper, Father."

"Oh!" cried Mabel, "just picked-off dandelions scattered all over an ocean of milk—how pretty!"

"We'll have the Village Improvement Society after us," laughed Marjory. "They don't allow a dandelion to show its head."

"I love dandelions," said Miss Blossom; "real ones, I mean; they're such gay, cheerful things and such a beautiful color."

"I love them, too," said Jean, "because, you know, they paid our rent for us."

"But," said Mabel, "I'm thankful we haven't got to dig all these dandelions."

"Now," said Miss Blossom, "we must go right to work. If everybody will help, Father and I will put it on for you. You needn't be afraid to trust us, because last spring we papered our two biggest rooms, and they really looked almost professional except for one strip that Father got upside-down; but your dining-room will be in no danger on that score, for Father never makes the same mistake twice. Jean, you and Mabel can move all the furniture except the table and sideboard into the kitchen—we'll have to stand on the table. Bettie, take down all the pictures. Father, you can be trimming the ceiling paper here on the sideboard while Marjory starts a fire in the kitchen stove so I can have hot water for my paste. We'll have our wall covered with dandelions in just no time!"

"Now," said Mr. Blossom, when the furniture was out and the pictures were all down, "we must dig the soil up well or our dandelions won't grow. Everybody must tear as much as she can of this old paper off the wall; it's so ragged it comes off very easily."

"The roof used to leak," said Bettie, "but my brother Rob unrolled some tin cans and nailed them over the place where the truly shingles are gone, and it never leaked a mite the last four times it rained."

"The plaster seems fairly good," said Mr. Blossom. "I could mend these holes with a little plaster of Paris if some obliging young lady would run with this dime to the drugstore for ten cents' worth."

"I'll go," said Mabel. "I don't think I like peeling walls."

"Mabel," said Miss Blossom, "isn't really fond of work, though I notice that she usually does her share."

Everybody helped to mend the cracks, and everybody watched with breathless interest to see the first long strip, upheld by Mr. Blossom and guided by Miss Blossom and the cottage broom, go into place.

"Wouldn't it be awful," whispered Mabel, "if it shouldn't stick?"

But it did stick, smooth and flat, and the paper was even prettier on the wall than it had been in the roll.

"A side strip next, Father, so we can see how it's going to look," pleaded Miss Blossom. "Remember, we're just children."

At five o'clock, when half of the ceiling and one side of the wall were finished, the front door was opened abruptly.

"Hi there!" said Mr. Black, putting his head in at the dining-room door. "Why don't you listen when I ring your bell? Is that dinner of mine ready? I'm losing a pound a day."

"No," said Bettie, jumping down from her perch on the sideboard, "but it will be next Friday. We're getting it ready just as fast as ever we can. We're even papering the dining-room for the occasion."

"Well," said Mr. Black, "I just stopped in to say that unless you could give me that dinner this very minute, I shall have to go hungry for the next five weeks."

"Oh!" cried Bettie, in dismay, "why?"

"Because I'm going to Washington tonight by the six o'clock train and I shall be gone a whole month—perhaps longer."

"Oh, dear," cried Bettie, "we just couldn't have you tonight. We're papering the dining-room, and besides we haven't a single thing to eat but some stale cake that Mrs. Pike gave us."

"I strongly suspect," said Mr. Black, smiling over Bettie's head at Mr. Blossom, "that you don't really want me to dinner."

"Oh, we do, we do," assured Bettie, earnestly, "but we just can't have company tonight. If you'll just let us know exactly when you're coming home, you'll find a beautiful dinner ready for you."

"All right," said Mr. Black, "I'll telegraph. I'll say: 'My dear Miss Bettykins, of Dandelion Cottage: It will give me great pleasure to dine with you tomorrow—or would you rather have me say the day after tomorrow?—evening. Yours most devotedly and-so-forth.'"

"Yes, yes," cried Bettie, "that will be all right, but you must give us three days to get ready in."

After all, however, it was Mabel that sent the telegram, and it was a very different one.

CHAPTER 9.
CHANGES AND PLANS

When the little dining-room was finished it was quite the prettiest room in the house, for the friendly Blossoms had painted the battered woodwork a delicate green to match the leaves in the paper; and by mixing what was left of the green paint with the remaining color left from the sideboard, clever Miss Blossom obtained a shade that was exactly right for as much of the floor as the rug did not cover. Of course all the neighbors and all the girls' relatives had to come in afterwards to see what Bettie called "the very dandelioniest room in Dandelion Cottage."

It seemed to the girls that the time fairly galloped from Monday to Thursday. They were heartily sorry when the moment came for them to lose their pleasant lodger. They went to the train to see the last of her and to assure her for the thousandth time that they should never forget her. Mabel sobbed audibly at the moment of parting, and large tears were rolling down silent Bettie's cheeks. Even the seven dollars and fifty cents that the girls had handled with such delight that morning paled into insignificance beside the fact that the train was actually whisking their beloved Miss Blossom away from them.

When she had paid for her lodging she advised her four landladies to deposit the money in the bank until time for the dinner party, and the girls did so, but even the importance of owning a bank account failed to console them for their loss. The train out of sight, the sober little procession wended its way to Dandelion Cottage but the cozy little house seemed strangely silent and deserted when Bettie unlocked the door. Mabel, who had wept stormily all the way home, sat down heavily on the doorstep and wept afresh.

Pinned to a pillow on the parlor couch, Jean discovered a little folded square of paper addressed to Bettie, who was drumming a sad little tune on the window pane.

"Why, Bettie," cried Jean, "this looks like a note for you from Miss Blossom! Do read it and tell us what she says."

"It says," read Bettie: "'My dearest of Betties: Thank you for being so nice to me. There's a telephone message for you.'"

"I wonder what it means," said Marjory.

Bettie ran to the talkless telephone, slipped her hand inside the little door at the top, and found a small square parcel wrapped in tissue paper, tied with a pink ribbon, and addressed to Miss Bettie Tucker, Dandelion Cottage. Bettie hastily undid the wrappings and squealed with delight when she saw the lovely little handkerchief, bordered delicately with lace, that Miss Blossom herself had made for her. There was a daintily embroidered "B" in the corner to make it Bettie's very own.

Marjory happened upon Jean's note peeping out from under a book on the parlor table. It said: "Dear Jean: Don't you think it's time for you to look at the kitchen clock?"

Of course everybody rushed to the kitchen to see Jean take from inside the case of the tickless clock a lovely handkerchief just like Bettie's except that it was marked with "J."

Marjory's note, which she presently found growing on the crimson petunia, sent her flying to the grindless coffee-mill, where she too found a similar gift.

"Well," said Mabel, who was now fairly cheerful, "I wonder if she forgot all about me."

For several anxious moments the girls searched eagerly in Mabel's behalf but no note was visible.

"I can't think where it could be," said housewifely Jean, stooping to pick up a bit of string from the dining-room rug, and winding it into a little ball. "I've looked in every room and—Why! what a long string! I wonder where it's all coming from."

"Under the rug," said Marjory, making a dive for the bit of paper that dangled from the end of the string. "Here's your note, Mabel."

"I think," Miss Blossom had written, "that there must be a mouse in the pantry mousetrap by this time."

"Yes!" shouted Mabel, a moment later. "A lovely lace-edged mouse with an 'M' on it—no, it's 'M B'—a really truly monogram, the very first monogram I ever had."

"Why, so it is," said Marjory. "I suppose she did that so we could tell them apart, because if she'd put M on both of them we wouldn't have known which was which."

"Why," cried Jean, "it's nearly an hour since the train left. Wasn't it sweet of her to think of keeping us interested so we shouldn't be quite so lonesome?"

"Yes," said Bettie, "it was even nicer than our lovely presents, but it was just like her."

"Oh, dear," said Mabel, again on the verge of tears, "I wish she might have stayed forever. What's the use of getting lovely new friends if you have to go and lose them the very next minute? She was just the nicest grown-up little girl there ever was, and I'll never see—see her any—"

"Look out, Mabel," warned Marjory, "if you cry on that handkerchief you'll spoil that monogram. Miss Blossom didn't intend these for crying-handkerchiefs—one good-sized tear would soak them."

Miss Blossom was not the only friend the girls were fated to lose that week. Grandma Pike, as everybody called the pleasant little old lady, was their next-door neighbor on the west side, and the cottagers were very fond of her. No one dreamed that Mrs. Pike would ever think of going to another town to live; but about ten days before Miss Blossom departed, the cheery old lady had quite taken everybody's breath away by announcing that she was going west, just as soon as she could get her things packed, to live with her married daughter.

When the girls heard that Grandma Pike was going away they were very much surprised and not at all pleased at the idea of losing one of their most delightful neighbors. At Miss Blossom's suggestion, they had spent several evenings working on a parting gift for their elderly friend. The gift, a wonderful linen traveling case with places in it to carry everything a traveler would be likely to need, was finished at last—with so many persons working on it, it was hard to keep all the pieces together—and the girls carried it to Grandma Pike, who seemed very much pleased.

"Well, well," said the delighted old lady, unrolling the parcel, "if you haven't gone and made me a grand slipper-bag! I'll think of you, now, every time I put on my slippers."

"No, no," protested Jean. "It's a traveling case with places in it for 'most everything but slippers."

"We all sewed on it," explained Mabel. "Those little bits of stitches that you can't see at all are Bettie's. Jean did all this feather-stitching, and Marjory hemmed all the binding. Miss Blossom basted it together so it wouldn't be crooked."

"What did you do, Mabel?" asked Grandma Pike, smiling over her spectacles.

"I took out the basting threads and embroidered these letters on the pockets."

"What does this 'P' stand for?"

"Pins," said Mabel. "You see it was sort of an accident. I started to embroider the word soap on this little pocket, but when I got the S O A done, there wasn't any room left for the P, so I just put it on the next pocket. I knew that if I explained that it was the end of 'Soap' and the beginning of 'Pins' you'd remember not to get your pins and soap mixed up."

During the lonely days immediately following Miss Blossom's departure, Mrs. Bartholomew Crane proved a great solace. The girls had somewhat neglected her during the preceding busy weeks; but with Miss Blossom gone, the cottagers became conscious of an aching void that new wall paper and lace handkerchiefs and a bank account could not quite fill; so presently they resumed their former habit of trotting across the street many times a day to visit good-natured Mrs. Crane.

Mrs. Crane's house was very small and looked rather gloomy from the outside because the paint had long ago peeled off and the weatherbeaten boards had grown black with age; but inside it was cheerfulness personified. First, there was Mrs. Crane herself, fairly radiating comfort. Then there was a bright rag carpet on the floor, a glowing red cloth on the little table, a lively yellow canary named Dicksy in one window, and a gorgeous red-and-crimson but very bad-tempered parrot in the other. There were only three rooms downstairs and two bed-chambers upstairs. Mrs. Crane's own room opened off the little parlor, and visitors could see the high feather bed always as smooth and rounded on top as one of Mrs. Crane's big loaves of light bread. The privileged girls were never tired of examining the good woman's patchwork quilts, made many years ago of minute, quaint, old-fashioned scraps of calico.

Even the garden seemed to differ from other gardens, for every inch of it except the patch of green grass under the solitary cherry tree was given over to flowers, many of them as quaint and old-fashioned as the bits of calico in the quilts, and to vegetables that ripened a week earlier for Mrs. Crane than similar varieties did for anyone else. Yet the garden was so little, and the variety so great, that Mrs. Crane never had enough of any one thing to sell. She owned her little home, but very little else. The two upstairs rooms were rented to lodgers, and she knitted stockings and mittens to sell because she could knit without using her eyes, which, like so many soft, bright, black eyes, were far from strong; but the little income so gained was barely enough to keep stout, warm-hearted, overgenerous Mrs. Crane supplied with food and fuel. The neighbors often wondered what would become of the good, lonely woman if she lost her lodgers, if her eyes failed completely, or if she should fall ill. Everybody agreed that Mrs. Crane should have been a wealthy woman instead of a poor one, because she would undoubtedly have done so much good with her money. Mabel had heard her father say that there was a good-sized mortgage on the place, and Dr. Bennett had instantly added: "Now, don't you say anything about that, Mabel." But ever after that, Mabel had kept her eyes open during her visits to Mrs. Crane, hoping to get a glimpse of the dreadful large-sized thing that was not to be mentioned.

On one occasion she thought she saw light. Mrs. Crane had expressed a fear that a wandering polecat had made a home under her woodshed.

"Is mortgage another name for polecat?" Mabel had asked a little later.

"No," imaginative Jean had replied. "A mortgage is more like a great, lean, hungry, gray wolf waiting just around the corner to eat you up. Don't ever use the word before Mrs. Crane; she has one."

"Where does she keep it?" demanded Mabel, agog with interest.

"I promised not to talk about it," said Jean, "and I won't."

Miss Blossom had been gone only two days when something happened to Mrs. Crane. It was none of the things that the neighbors had expected to happen, but for a little while it looked almost as serious. Bettie, running across the street right after breakfast one morning, with a bunch of fresh chickweed for the yellow canary and a cracker for cross Polly, found Mrs. Crane, usually the most cheerful person imaginable, sitting in her kitchen with a swollen, crimson foot in a pail of lukewarm water, and groaning dismally.

"Oh, Mrs. Crane!" cried surprised Bettie. "What in the world is the matter? Are—are you coming down with anything?"

"I've already come," moaned Mrs. Crane, grimly. "I was out in my back yard in my thin old slippers early this morning putting hellebore on my currant bushes, and I stepped down hard on the teeth of the rake that I'd dropped on the grass. There's two great holes in my foot. How I'm ever going to do things I don't know, for 'twas all I could do to crawl into the house on my hands and knees."

"Isn't there something I can do for you?" asked Bettie, sympathetically.

"Could you get a stick of wood from the shed and make me a cup of tea? Maybe I'd feel braver if I wasn't so empty."

"Of course I could," said Bettie, cheerily.

"I tell you what it is," confided Mrs. Crane. "It's real nice and independent living all alone as long as you're strong and well, but just the minute anything happens, there you are like a Robinson Crusoe, cast away on a desert isle. I began to think nobody would ever come."

"Can't I do something more for you?" asked Bettie, poking scraps of paper under the kettle to bring it to a boil. "Don't you want Dr. Bennett to look at your foot? Hadn't I better get him?"

"Yes, do," said Mrs. Crane, "and then come back. I can't bear to think of staying here alone."

For the next four days there was a deep depression in the middle of Mrs. Crane's puffy feather bed, for the injured foot was badly swollen and Mrs. Crane was far too heavy to go hopping about on the other one. At first, her usually hopeful countenance wore a strained, anxious expression, quite pathetic to see.

"Now don't you worry one bit," said comforting little Bettie. "We'll take turns staying with you; we'll feed Polly and Dicksy, and I believe every friend you have is going to offer to make broth. Mother's making some this minute."

"But there's the lodgers," groaned Mrs. Crane, "both as particular as a pair of old maids in a glass case. Mr. Barlow wants his bedclothes tucked in all around so tight that a body'd think he was afraid of rolling out of bed nights, and Mr. Bailey won't have his tucked in at all—says he likes 'em 'floating round loose and airy.' Do you suppose you girls can make those two beds and not get those two lodgers mixed up? I declare, I'm so absent-minded myself that I've had to climb those narrow stairs many a day to make sure I'd done it right."

"Don't be afraid," said Jean, who had joined Bettie. "Marjory's Aunty Jane has taught her to make beds beautifully, and I have a good memory. Between us we'll manage splendidly."

"But there's my garden," mourned the usually busy woman, who found it hard to lie still with folded hands in a world that seemed to be constantly needing her. "Dear me! I don't see how I'm going to spare myself for a whole week just when everything is growing so fast."

"We'll tend to the garden, too," promised Bettie.

"Yes, indeed we will," echoed Mabel. "We'll water everything and weed—"

"No, you won't," said Mrs. Crane, quickly. "You can do all the watering you like, but if I catch any of you weeding, there'll be trouble."

The young cottagers were even better than their promises, for they took excellent care of Mrs. Crane, the lodgers, the parrot, the canary, and the garden, until the injured foot was well again; but while doing all this they learned something that distressed them very much, indeed. Of course they had always known in a general way that their friend was far from being wealthy, but they had not guessed how touchingly poor she really was. But now they saw that her cupboard was very scantily filled, that her clothing was very much patched and mended, her shoes distressingly worn out, and that even her dish-towels were neatly darned.

"But we won't talk about it to people," said fine-minded Jean. "Perhaps she wouldn't like to have everybody know."

Even Jean, however, did not guess what a comfort proud Mrs. Crane had found it to have her warm-hearted little friends stand between her poverty and the sometimes-too-prying eyes of a grown-up world.

Unobservant though they had seemed, the girls did not forget about the Mother-Hubbardlike state of Mrs. Crane's cupboard. After that one of their finest castles in Spain always had Mrs. Crane, who would have made such a delightful mother and who had never had any children, enthroned as its gracious mistress. When they had time to think about it at all, it always grieved them to think of their generous-natured, no-longer-young friend dreading a poverty-stricken, love-less, and perhaps homeless old age; for this, they had discovered, was precisely what Mrs. Crane was doing.

"If she were a little, thin, active old lady, with bobbing white curls like Grandma Pike," said Jean, "lots of people would have a corner for her; but poor Mrs. Crane takes up so much room and is so heavy and slow that she's going to be hard to take care of when she gets old. Oh, why couldn't she have had just one strong, kind son to take care of her?"

"When I'm married," offered Mabel, generously, "I'll take her to live with me. I won't have any husband if he doesn't promise to take Mrs. Crane, too."

"You shan't have her," declared Jean. "I want her myself."

"She's already promised to me," said Bettie, triumphantly. "We're going to keep house together some place, and I'm going to be an old-maid kindergarten teacher."

"I don't think that's fair, Bettie Tucker," said Marjory, earnestly. "I don't see how my children are to have any grandmother if she doesn't live with me. Imagine the poor little things with Aunty Jane for a grandmother!"

CHAPTER 10.
THE MILLIGANS

To the moment of Grandma Pike's departure, all their neighbors had been so pleasant that the girls were deceived into thinking that neighbors were never anything but pleasant. Although they felt not the slightest misgiving as to their future neighbors, they had hated to lose dear old Grandma Pike, who had always been as good to them as if she had really been their grandmother, and whose parting gifts—sundry odds and ends of dishes, old magazines, and broken parcels of provisions—gave them occupation for many delightful days. In spite of the lasting pleasure of this unexpected donation, however, they could not help feeling that, with Mr. Black away, Miss Blossom gone, Mrs. Pike living in another town, and only disabled Mrs. Crane left, they were losing friends with alarming rapidity. Grief for the departed, however, did not prevent their taking an active interest in the persons who were to occupy the house next door, which Mrs. Pike's departure had left vacant.

"I wonder," said Marjory, pulling the curtain back to get a better view of the empty house, "what the new people will be like. It's exciting, isn't it, to have something happening in this quiet neighborhood? What did Grandma Pike say the name was?"

"Milligan," replied Bettie.

"Kind of nice name, isn't it?" asked Jean.

"Yes," agreed Mabel, brightening suddenly. "I made up a long, long rhyme about it last night before I went to sleep. Want to hear it?"

"Of course."

"This one really rhymes," explained Mabel, importantly. Her verses sometimes lacked that desirable quality, so when they did rhyme Mabel always liked to mention it. "Here it is:

> *"As soon as a man named Milligan*
> *Got well he always fell ill again—ill again—ill—*

"Dear me, I can't remember how it went. There was a lot more, but I've forgotten the rest."

"It's a great pity," said Marjory, drily, "that you didn't forget all of it, because if there's really a Mr. Milligan, and I ever see him, I'll think of that rhyme and I won't be able to keep my face straight."

"We must be very polite to the Milligans," said considerate Bettie, "and call on them as soon as they come. Mother always calls on new people; she says it makes folks feel more comfortable to be welcomed into the neighborhood."

"Mrs. Crane does it, too. We're the nearest, perhaps we ought to be the first."

"I think," suggested Jean thoughtfully, "we'd better wait until they're nicely settled; they might not like visitors too soon. You know we didn't."

"They're going to move in today," said Mabel. "Goodness! I wish they'd hurry and come; I'm so excited that I keep dusting the same shelf over and over again. I'm just wild to see them!"

It was sweeping-day at the cottage when the Milligans' furniture began to arrive, but it looked very much as if the sweeping would last for at least two days because the girls were unable to get very far away from the windows that faced west. These were the bedroom windows, and, as there were only two of them, there were usually two heads at each window.

"There comes the first load," announced Marjory, at last. "There's a high-chair on the very top, so there must be a baby."

"I'm so glad," said Bettie. "I just love a baby."

Two men unpacked the Milligans' furniture in the Milligans' front yard, and each load seemed more interesting than the one before it. It was such fun to guess what the big, clumsy parcels contained, particularly when the contents proved to be quite different from what the girls expected.

"Somehow, I don't think they're going to be very nice people," said Mabel. "I b'lieve we're going to be disappointed in 'em."

"Why, Mabel," objected Jean, "we don't know a thing about them yet."

"Yes, I do too. Their things—look—they don't look ladylike."

"Oh, Mabel," laughed Marjory, "you're so funny."

"Perhaps," offered Jean, "the Milligans are poor and the children have spoiled things."

"No," insisted Mabel. "They've got some of the newest and shiningest furniture I ever saw, but I b'lieve it's imitation."

"Oh, Mabel," laughed Jean, "I hope you won't watch the loads when I move. For a girl that's slept for three weeks on an imitation pillow, you're pretty critical."

Presently the Milligans themselves arrived. Mabel happened to be counting the buds on the poppy plants when they came.

"Girls!" she cried, rushing into the cottage with the news. "They've come. I saw them all. There's a Mr. Milligan, a Mrs. Milligan, a girl, a boy, a baby, and a dog. The girl's the oldest. She's just about my size—I mean height—and she has straight, light hair. The baby walks, and none of them are so very good-looking."

It did not take the newcomers long to discover that their next-door neighbors were four little girls. Mrs. Milligan found it out that very afternoon when she went to the back door to borrow tea. Bettie explained, very politely, that Dandelion Cottage was only a playhouse, and that their tea-caddy contained nothing but glass beads. When Mrs. Milligan returned to her own house, she told her own family about it.

"You might as well run over and play with them, Laura," she said. "Take the baby with you, too. He's a dreadful nuisance under my feet. That'll be a real nice place for you both to play all summer."

The girls received their visitors pleasantly; almost, indeed, with enthusiasm; but after a very few moments, they began to eye the baby with apprehension. He refused to make friends with them but wandered about rather lawlessly and handled their treasures roughly. Laura paid no attention to him but talked to the girls. She seemed a bright girl and not at all bashful, and she used a great many slang phrases that sounded new and, it must be confessed, rather attractive to the girls.

"Oh, land, yes," she said, "we came here from Chicago where we had all kinds of money, and clothes to burn—we lived in a beautiful flat. Pa just came here to oblige Mr. Williams—he's going to clerk in Williams's store. Come over and see me—we'll be real friendly and have lots of good times together—I can put you up to lots of dodges. Say, this is a dandy place to play in—I'm coming over often."

Jean looked in silence at Bettie, Bettie at Mabel, and Mabel at Marjory. Surely such an outburst of cordiality deserved a fitting response, but no one seemed to be able to make it.

"Do," said Jean, finally, but rather feebly, "we'd be pleased to have you."

Except for a few lively but good-natured squabbles between Marjory, who was something of a tease, and Mabel, who was Marjory's favorite victim, the little mistresses of Dandelion Cottage had always played together in perfect harmony; but with the coming of the Milligans everything was changed.

To start with, between the Milligan baby and the Milligan dog, the girls knew no peace. Mrs. Milligan was right when she said that the baby was a nuisance, for it would have been hard to find a more troublesome three-year-old. He pulled down everything he could reach, broke the girls' best dishes, wiped their precious petunia and the geraniums completely out of existence, and roared with a deep bass voice if anyone attempted to interfere with him. The dog carried mud into the neat little cottage, scratched up the garden, and growled if the girls tried to drive him out.

"Well," said Mabel, disconsolately, in one of the rare moments when the girls were alone, "I could stand the baby and the dog. But I can't stand Laura!"

"Laura certainly likes to boss," said Bettie, who looked pale and worried. "I don't just see what we're going to do about it. I try to be nice to her, but I can't like her. Mother says we must be polite to her, but I don't believe Mother knows just what a queer girl she is—you see she's always as quiet as can be when there are grown people around."

"Yes," agreed Mabel, "her company manners are so much properer than mine that Mother says she wishes I were more like her."

"Well," said Marjory, uncompromisingly, "I'm mighty glad you're not. Your manners aren't particularly good, but you haven't two sets. I think Laura's the most disagreeable girl I ever knew. Just as she fools you into almost liking her, she turns around and scratches you."

"Perhaps," said Jean, "if her people were nicer—By the way, Mother says that after this we must keep the windows shut while Mr. Milligan is splitting wood in his back yard so we can't hear the awful things he says, and that if we hear Mr. and Mrs. Milligan quarreling again we mustn't listen."

"Listen!" exclaimed Mabel. "We don't need to listen. Their voices keep getting louder and louder until it seems as if they were right in this house."

"Of course," said Marjory, "it can't be pleasant for Laura at home, but, dear me, it isn't pleasant for us with her over here."

Badly-brought-up Laura was certainly not a pleasant playmate. She wanted to lead in everything and was amiable only when she was having her own way. She was not satisfied with the way the cottage was arranged but rearranged it to suit herself. She told the girls that their garments were countrified, and laughed scornfully at Bettie's boyish frocks and heavy shoes. She ridiculed rotund Mabel for being fat, and said that Marjory's nose turned up and that Jean's rather large mouth was a good opening for a young dentist. Before the first week was fairly over, the four girls—who had lived so happily before her arrival—were grieved, indignant, or downright angry three-fourths of the time.

Laura had one habit that annoyed the girls excessively, although at first they had found it rather amusing. Later, however, owing perhaps to a certain rasping quality in Laura's voice, it grew very tiresome. She transposed the initials of their names. For instance, Bettie Tucker became Tettie Bucker, Jeanie Mapes became Meanie Japes, while Mabel became Babel Mennett. It was particularly distressing to have Laura speak familiarly in her sharp, half-scornful tones, of their dear, departed Miss Blossom, whose name was Gertrude, as Bertie Glossom. Mr. Peter Black, of course, became Beter Plack, and Mrs. Bartholomew Crane was Mrs. Cartholomew Brane, to lawless young Laura.

"I don't think it's exactly respectful to do that to grown-up people's names," protested Bettie, one day.

"Pooh!" said Laura. "Mrs. Cartholomew Brane looks just like an old washtub, she's so fat—who'd be respectful to a washtub? There goes Toctor Ducker, Tettie Bucker. Huh! I'd hate to be a parson's daughter—

they're always as poor as church mice. What did you say your mother's first name is?"

"I didn't say and I'm not going to," returned Bettie.

"Well, anyhow, her bonnet went out of style four years ago. I should think the parish'd take up a subscription and get her a new one."

"I wish, Laura," said exasperated Jean, another day, "that you wouldn't meddle with our things. This bedroom is mine and Bettie's, and the other one is Mabel's and Marjory's. We wouldn't think of looking into each other's private treasure boxes. I've seen you open mine half a dozen times this week. The things are all keepsakes and I'd rather not have them handled."

"Huh! I guess I'll handle 'em if I want to. My mother can't keep me out of her bureau drawers, and I don't think you're so very much smarter."

A day or two later, the girls of Dandelion Cottage were invited to a party in another portion of the town. The invitations were left at their own cottage door and the delighted girls began at once to make plans for the party.

"Let's carry our new handkerchiefs," suggested Jean, going to her treasure box. "I believe I'll take mine home with me—I dreamed last night that the cottage was on fire and that mine got burned. Besides, I'll have to get dressed at home for the party and it would be handier to have it there."

"Guess I will, too," said Bettie.

"Great idea," said Marjory, taking her own box from its shelf. "I never should have thought of anything so bright. Let's all write to Miss Blossom and tell her that we carried our—Why! mine isn't in my box!"

"Neither is mine," cried Mabel, who had turned quite pale at the discovery. "It was there this morning. Girls, did any of you touch our handkerchiefs?"

"Of course we didn't," said Jean. "See, here's mine with 'J' on it, and there are no others in my box."

"Of course not," echoed Laura.

"Mine's here, all right," said Bettie, who had been struggling with her box, which opened hard. "Are you sure you left them in your boxes?"

"Certain sure," replied Mabel. "I saw it this morning."

"So did I see mine," asserted Marjory. "After I'd shown it to Aunty Jane I brought it back to put in my treasure box."

"Laura," asked Jean, "was Marjory's handkerchief in her box when you looked in it this morning? I heard the cover make that funny little clicking noise that it always makes, and just a minute afterward you came out of her room."

"I—I don't know," stammered Laura. "I didn't see it—I never touched her old box. If you say I did, I'll go right home and tell my mother you called me a thief. I'm going now, anyway."

The girls were in the dining-room just outside of the back bedroom door. As Laura was brushing past Jean, the opening of the new girl's blouse caught in such a fashion on the corner of the sideboard that the garment, which fastened in front, came unbuttoned from top to bottom. From its bulging front dropped Bettie's bead chain, various articles of doll's clothing, and the two missing handkerchiefs.

"They're mine!" cried Laura, making a dive for the things.

"They're not any such thing!" cried indignant Jean. "I made that doll's dress myself, and I know the lace on those handkerchiefs."

"They're my mother's," protested Laura. "I took 'em out of her drawer."

"They're not," contradicted Mabel, prying Laura's fingers apart and forcing her to drop one of the crumpled handkerchiefs. "Look at that monogram—'M B' for Mabel Bennett."

"It's no such thing," lied Laura, stoutly. "It stands for Bertha Milligan and that's my mother's name."

"Give me that other handkerchief this instant," demanded Jean, giving Laura a slight shake. "If you don't, we'll take it away from you."

"Take the old rag," said Laura. "My mother gives away better hand-kerchiefs than these to beggars. I just took 'em anyway to scare Varjory Male and Babel Mennett, the silly babies."

After this enlightening experience, the girls never for a moment left their unwelcome visitor alone in any of the rooms of Dandelion Cot-tage. They stood her for almost a week longer, principally because there seemed to be no way of getting rid of her. Mabel, indeed, had several lively quarrels with her during that time, because quick-tempered Mabel, always strictly truthful herself, could not tolerate deceit in anyone else, and she had, of course, lost all faith in Laura.

The end came suddenly one Friday afternoon. Miss Blossom had sent to the girls, by mail, a photograph of her own charming self, and nothing that the cottage contained was more precious. After one of the usual tiffs with Mabel, high-handed Laura spitefully scratched a dis-figuring mustache right across the beautiful face, ruining the priceless treasure beyond repair.

Even Laura looked slightly dismayed at the result of her spiteful work. The others for a moment were too horror-stricken for words. Then Mabel, with blazing eyes, sprang to her feet and flung the cottage door wide open.

"You go home, Laura Milligan!" she cried. "Don't you ever dare to come inside this house again!"

"Yes, go," cried mild Bettie, for once thoroughly roused. "We've tried to be nice to you and there hasn't been a single day that you haven't been rude and horrid. Go home this minute. We're done with you."

"I won't go until I'm good and ready," retorted Laura, tearing the disfigured photograph in two and scornfully tossing the pieces into a corner. "Such a fuss about a skinny old maid's picture."

"You shan't stay one instant longer!" cried indignant Jean, stepping determinedly behind Laura, placing her hands on the girl's shoulders, and making a sudden run for the door. "There! You're out. Don't you ever attempt to come in again."

Bettie, grasping the situation and the Milligan baby at the same time, promptly set the boy outside. She had handled him with the utmost gentleness, but he always roared if anyone touched him, and he roared now.

"Yah!" yelled Laura, "I'll tell my mother you pinched him—slapped him, too."

"Sapped him, too," wailed the baby.

"Well," said Jean, turning the key in the lock, "we'll have to keep the door locked after this. Mercy! I never behaved so dreadfully to anybody before and I hope I'll never have to again."

CHAPTER 11.
AN EMBARRASSING VISITOR

Up to the time of the unpleasantness with Laura, the girls had unlocked the cottage in the morning and had left it unlocked until they were ready to go home at night, for the girls spent all their waking hours at Dandelion Cottage. Bettie, indeed, had the care of the youngest two Tucker babies, but they were good little creatures and when the girls played with their dolls they were glad to include the two placid babies, just as if they too were dolls. The littlest baby, in particular, made a remarkably comfortable plaything, for it was all one to him whether he slept in Jean's biggest doll's cradle, or in the middle of the dining-room table, as long as he was permitted to sleep sixteen hours out of the twenty-four. When he wasn't asleep, he sucked his thumb contentedly, crowed happily on one of the cottage beds, or rolled cheerfully about on the cottage floor. The older baby, too, obligingly stayed wherever the girls happened to put him. After this experience with the Tucker infants, the Milligan baby had proved a great disappointment to the girls, for they had hoped to use him, too, as an animated doll;

but he had refused steadfastly to make friends even with Bettie, whose way with babies was something beautiful to see.

The girls were all required to do their own mending, but they found it no hardship to do their darning on their own doorstep on sunny days, or around the dining-room table if the north wind happened to be blowing, for they always had so many interesting things to talk about.

During the daytime, the cottage was never left entirely alone. It was occupied even at mealtimes because the four families dined and supped at different hours; for instance, Marjory's Aunty Jane always liked her tea at half-past five, but Jean's people did not dine until seven. Owing to the impossibility of capturing all the boys at one time, supper at the Tucker house was a movable feast, so Bettie usually ate whenever she found it most convenient. As for Mabel, it is doubtful if she knew the exact hours for meals at the Bennett house because she was invariably late. After the handkerchief episode, the girls planned that one or another of them should always be in the cottage from the time that it was opened in the morning until it was again locked for the night. The morning after the later quarrel, however, the girls met by previous arrangement on Mabel's doorstep, went in a body to the cottage, and, after they were all inside, carefully locked the door.

"We'll be on the safe side, anyway," said Jean. "Though I shouldn't think that Laura would ever want to come near the place again."

"Oh, she'll come fast enough," said Mabel. "She's cheeky enough for anything. Do you s'pose she told her mother about it? She said she was going to."

"Pshaw!" said Marjory. "She was always threatening to tell her mother, but nothing ever came of it. If she'd told her mother half the things she said she was going to, she wouldn't have had time to eat or sleep."

It was hopeless, the girls had decided, to attempt to mend the ruined photograph, so, at Bettie's suggestion, they had sorrowfully cut it into four pieces of equal size, which they divided between them. They had just laid the precious fragments tenderly away in their treasure boxes when the doorbell rang with such a loud, prolonged, jangling peal that everybody jumped.

"Laura!" exclaimed the four girls.

"No," said Jean, cautiously drawing back the curtain of the front window and peeping out. "It's Mrs. Milligan!"

"Goodness!" whispered Marjory, "there's no knowing what Laura told her—she never did tell anything straight."

"Let's keep still," said Mabel. "Perhaps she'll think there's nobody home."

"No hope of that," said Jean. "She saw us come in. But, pshaw! she can't hurt us anyway."

"No," said Marjory. "What's the use of being afraid? We didn't do anything to be ashamed of. Aunty Jane says we should have turned Laura out the day she took the handkerchiefs."

"I'm not exactly afraid," said Bettie, "but I don't like Mrs. Milligan. Still, we'll have to let her in, I suppose."

A second vigorous peal at the bell warned them that their visitor was getting impatient.

"You're the biggest and the most dignified," said Marjory, giving Jean a shove. "You go."

"Don't ask her in if you can help it," warned Bettie, in a pleading whisper. "The doorbell sounds as if she didn't like us very well."

But the visitor did not wait to be asked to come in. The moment Jean turned the key the door was flung open and Mrs. Milligan brushed past the astonished quartet and sailed into the parlor, where she seated herself bolt upright on the cozy corner.

"I'd like to know," demanded Mrs. Milligan, in a hard, cold tone that fell unpleasantly on the cottagers' ears, "if you consider it ladylike for four great overgrown girls to pitch into one poor innocent little child and a helpless baby? Your conduct yesterday was simply outrageous. You might have injured those children for life, or even broken the baby's back."

"Broken the baby's back!" gasped Bettie, in honest amazement. "Why, I simply lifted him with my two hands and set him just outside the door. I never was rough with any baby in all my life!"

"I happen to know, on excellent authority," said Mrs. Milligan, "that you slapped both of those helpless children and threw them down the front steps. Laura was so excited about it that she couldn't sleep, and the poor baby cried half the night—we fear that he's injured internally."

"Nobody here injured him," said Mabel. "He always cries all the time, anyhow."

"We did put them out and for a very good reason," said Jean, speaking as respectfully as she could, "but we certainly didn't hurt either of them. I'm sorry if the baby isn't well, but I know it isn't our fault."

"Laura walked down the steps," said Bettie, "and the baby turned over and slid down on his stomach the way he always does."

"I should think that a minister's daughter," said Mrs. Milligan, with a withering glance at poor shrinking Bettie, "would scorn to tell such lies."

Bettie, who had never before been accused of untruthfulness, looked the picture of conscious guilt; a tide of crimson flooded her cheeks and she fingered the buttons on her blouse nervously. She was too dumbfounded to speak a word in her own defense. Mabel, however, was only too ready.

"Bettie never told a lie in her life," cried the indignant little girl. "It was your own Laura that told stories if anybody did—and I guess somebody did, all right. Laura never tells the truth; she doesn't know how to."

"I have implicit confidence in Laura," returned Mrs. Milligan, frowning at Mabel. "I believe every word she says."

"Well," retorted dauntless Mabel, "that's more than the rest of us do. We kept count one day and she told seventy-two fibs that we know of."

"Oh, Mabel, do hush," pleaded scandalized Bettie.

"Hush nothing," said Mabel, not to be deterred. "I'm only telling the truth. Laura took our handkerchiefs and then fibbed about it, and we've missed a dozen things since that she probably carried off and—"

"Mabel, Mabel!" warned Jean, pressing her hand over Mabel's too reckless lips. "Don't you know that we decided not to say a word about those other things? They didn't amount to anything, and we'd rather have peace than to make a fuss about them."

"I can see very plainly," said Mrs. Milligan, with cold disapproval, "that you're not at all the proper sort of children for my little Laura to play with. I forbid you to speak to her again; I don't care to have her associate with you. I can believe all she says about you, for I've never been treated so rudely in my life."

"Apologize, Mabel," whispered Jean, whose arm was still about the younger girl's neck.

"If I was rude," said candid Mabel, "I beg your pardon. I didn't mean to be impolite, but every word I said about Laura was true."

"I shall not accept your apology," said Mrs. Milligan, rising to depart, "until you've sent a written apology to Laura and have retracted everything you've said about her, besides."

"It'll never be accepted then," said quick-tempered Mabel, "for we haven't done anything to apologize for."

"No, Mrs. Milligan," said Jean, in her even, pleasant voice. "No apology to Laura can ever come from us. We stood her just as long as we could, and then we turned her out just as kindly as anyone could have done it. I told Mother all about it last night and she agreed that there wasn't anything else we could have done."

"So did Mamma," said Bettie.

"So did Aunty Jane."

"Well," said Mrs. Milligan, pausing on the porch, "I'd thank you young gossips to keep your tongues and your hands off my children in the future."

Jean closed the door and the four girls looked at one another in silence. None of their own relatives were at all like Mrs. Milligan and they didn't know just what to make of their unpleasant experience. At last, Marjory gave a long sigh.

"Well," said she, "I came awfully near telling her when she forbade our playing with Laura that my Aunty Jane has forbidden me to even speak to her poor abused Laura."

"As for me," said Mabel, with lofty scorn, "I don't need to be forbidden."

"Come, girls," said Jean, "I'm sorry it had to happen, but I'm glad the matter's ended. Let's not talk about it any more. Let's have one of our own good old happy days—the kind we had before Laura came."

"I'll tell you what we'll do," said Bettie. "We'll each write out a bill of fare for Mr. Black's dinner party, and we'll see how many different things we can think of. In that way, we'll be sure not to forget anything."

"But the Milligans," breathed Marjory, promptly seeing through Bettie's tactful scheme.

The Milligan matter, however, was not by any means ended. It was true that the girls paid no further attention to Laura, but this did not deter that rather vindictive young person from annoying the little cottagers in every way that she possibly could, although she was afraid to work openly.

As Laura knew, the girls took great pride in their little garden. Bettie's good-natured big brother Rob had offered to take care of their tiny lawn, and he kept it smooth and even. The round pansy bed daily yielded handfuls of great purple, white, or golden blossoms; the thrifty nasturtiums were beginning to bloom with creditable freedom; and many of the different, prettily foliaged little plants in the long bed near the Milligans' fence were opening their first curious, many-colored flowers.

Some of the vegetables were positively getting radishes and carrots on their roots, as Bettie put it. The pride of the vegetable garden, however, was a huge, rampant vine that threatened to take possession of the entire yard. There was just the one plant; no one knew where the seed came from or how it had managed to get itself planted, but there it was, close beside the back fence. For want of a better name, the girls called it "The Accident," and they expected wonderful things from it when the great yellow trumpet-shaped flowers should give place to fruit, although they didn't know in the least what kind of crop to look for. But this made it all the more delightful.

"Perhaps it'll be pumpkins," said Jean. "I guess I'd better hunt up a recipe for pumpkin pie, so's to be ready when the time comes."

"Or those funny, pale green squashes that are scalloped all around the edge like a dish," said Marjory.

"Or cucumbers," said Bettie. "I took Mrs. Crane a leaf, one day, and she said it might be cucumbers."

"Or watermelons," said Mabel. "Um-m! wouldn't it be grand if it should happen to be watermelons?"

"What I'm wondering is," said Jean, "whether there's any danger of the vine's going around the house and taking possession of the front yard, too. I could almost believe that this was a seedling of Jack's beanstalk except that it runs on the ground instead of up."

"If it tries to go around the corner," laughed Bettie, "we'll train it up the back of the house. Wouldn't it be fun to have pumpkins, or squashes, or cucumbers, or melons, or maybe all of them at once, growing on our roof?"

The day after Mrs. Milligan's visit, Laura, who was not invited to the party, and who found time heavy on her hands, watched the girls, after stopping for Marjory, set out in their pretty summer dresses to spend the afternoon at a young friend's house. Laura gazed after them enviously. There was no reason why she should have been invited, for she had never met the little girl who was giving the party, but she didn't think of that. Instead, she foolishly laid the unintentional slight at the little cottagers' door.

Mrs. Milligan was sewing on the doorstep and had given Laura a dish-towel to hem. Saying something about hunting for a thimble, Laura went to the kitchen, took the bread-knife from the table drawer, stole quietly out of the back door, and slipped between the bars of the back fence. Reaching the splendid vine that the girls loved so dearly, she parted the huge, rough leaves until she found the spot where the vine started from the ground. First looking about cautiously to make certain that no one was in sight, spiteful Laura drew the knife back and forth across the thick stem until, with a sudden, sharp crack, the sturdy vine parted from its root.

Two minutes later, Laura, looking the picture of propriety, sat on the Milligans' doorstep hemming her dish-towel.

Of course, when the girls made their next daily excursion about their garden they were almost broken-hearted at finding their beloved vine flat on the ground, all withered and dead.

"Oh," mourned Marjory, "now we'll never know what 'The Accident' was going to bear, pumpkins or squashes or—"

"Yes," said Mabel, who was blinking hard to keep the tears back, "that's the hardest part of it, it was cut off in its p-prime—Oh, dear, I guess I'm g-going to cry."

"What could have done it?" asked Bettie, who was not far from following Mabel's example. "Has anyone stepped on it?"

"Perhaps a potato bug ate it off," suggested Jean.

"A two-legged potato bug, I guess," said Marjory, who had been examining the ground carefully. "See, here are small sharp heel prints close to the root."

"Whose handkerchief is this?" asked Mabel, picking up a small tightly crumpled ball and unrolling it gingerly. "There's a name on it but my eyes are so teary I can't make it out."

"It looks like Milligan," said Bettie, turning it over, "but we can't tell how long it's been here."

"Horrid as she is," said charitable Jean, "it doesn't seem as if even Laura would do such a mean thing. I can't believe it of her."

"I can," said Mabel. "If she had a squash vine, or a pumpkin vine, I'd go straight over and spoil it this minute."

"No, no," said Jean, "we mustn't be horrid just because other folks are. We won't pay any attention to her—we'll just be patient."

The girls found four small, green, egglike objects growing on the withered vine; they cut them off and these, too, were laid tenderly away in their treasure boxes.

"When we get old," said Mabel, tearfully, "we'll take 'em out and tell our grandchildren all about 'The Accident.'"

But even this prospect did not quite console the girls for the loss of their treasure.

For the next few days, Laura remained contented with doing on the sly whatever she could to annoy the girls. One evening, when the girls had gone home for the night and while her mother was away from home, Laura threw a brick at one of the cottage windows, breaking a pane of glass. Reaching in through the hole, she scattered handfuls of sand on the clean floor that the girls had scrubbed that morning. Another night she emptied a basketful of potato parings on their neat front porch and daubed molasses on their doorknob—mean little tricks prompted by a mean little nature.

It wasn't much fun, however, to annoy persons who refused to show any sign of being annoyed, and Laura presently changed her tactics. Taking a large bone from the pantry one day, when the girls were sitting on their doorstep, she first showed it to Towser, the Milligan dog, and then threw it over the fence into the very middle of the pansy bed. Of course, the big clumsy dog bounded over the low fence after the bone, crushing many of the delicate pansy plants. After that at regular intervals, Laura threw sticks and other bones into the other beds with very much the same result.

The next time Rob cut the grass he noticed the untidy appearance of the beds and asked the reason. The girls explained.

"I'll shoot that dog if you say so," offered Rob, with honest indignation.

"No, no," said Bettie, "it isn't the dog's fault."

"No," said Jean, "we're not sure that the dog isn't the least objectionable member of the Milligan family."

"How would it do if I licked the boy?" asked Rob.

"It wouldn't do at all," replied Bettie. "He works somewhere in the daytime and never even looks in this direction when he's home. He's afraid of girls."

"Then I guess you'll have to grin and bear it," said Rob, moving off with the lawn-mower, "since neither of my remedies seems to fit the case."

/

CHAPTER 12.
A LIVELY AFTERNOON

It happened one day that Mrs. Milligan was obliged to spend a long afternoon at the dentist's, leaving Laura in charge of the house. Unfortunately it happened, too, that this was the day when the sewing society met, and Mrs. Tucker had asked Bettie to stay home for the afternoon because the next-to-the-youngest baby was ill with a croupy cold and could not go out of doors to the cottage. Devoted Jean offered to stay with her beloved Bettie, who gladly accepted the offer. Before going to Bettie's, however, Jean ran over to Dandelion Cottage to tell the other girls about it.

"Mabel," asked Jean, a little doubtfully, "are you quite sure you'll be able to turn a deaf ear if Laura should happen to bother you? I'm half afraid to leave you two girls here alone."

"You needn't be," said Mabel. "I wouldn't associate with Laura if I were paid for it. She isn't my kind."

"No," said Marjory, "you needn't worry a mite. We're going to sit on the doorstep and read a perfectly lovely book that Aunty Jane found at the library—it's one that she liked when she was a little girl. We're going to take turns reading it aloud."

"Well, that certainly ought to keep you out of mischief. You'll be safe enough if you stick to your book. If anything should happen, just remember that I'm at Bettie's."

"Yes, Grandma," said Marjory, with a comical grimace.

Jean laughed, ran around the house, and squeezed through the hole in the back fence.

Half an hour later, lonely Laura, discovering the girls on their doorstep, amused herself by sicking the dog at them. Towser, however, merely growled lazily for a few moments and then went to sleep in the sunshine—he, at least, cherished no particular grudge against the girls and probably by that time he recognized them as neighbors.

Then Laura perched herself on one of the square posts of the dividing fence and began to sing—in her high, rasping, exasperating voice—a song that was almost too personal to be pleasant. It had taken Laura almost two hours to compose it, some days before, and fully another hour to commit it to memory, but she sang it now in an offhand, haphazard way that led the girls to suppose that she was making it up as she went along. It ran thus:

> There's a lanky girl named Jean,
> Who's altogether too lean.
> Her mouth is too big,
> And she wears a wig,
> And her eyes are bright sea-green.

Of course it was quite impossible to read even a thrillingly interesting book with rude Laura making such a disturbance. If the girls had been wise, they would have gone into the house and closed the door, leaving Laura without an audience; but they were not wise and they were curious. They couldn't help waiting to hear what Laura was going to sing about the rest of them, and they did not need to wait long; Laura

LAURA, PERCHED HIGH ON THE FENCE-POST, BEGAN TO SING.

promptly obliged them with the second verse:

> There's another named Marjory Vale,
>
> Who's about the size of a snail.
>
> Her teeth are light blue—
>
> She hasn't but two—
>
> And her hair is much too pale.

Laura had, in several instances, sacrificed truth for the sake of rhyme, but enough remained to injure the vanity of the subjects of her song very sharply. Marjory breathed quickly for a moment and flushed pink but gave no audible sign that she had heard. Laura, somewhat disappointed, proceeded:

> There's a silly young lass called Bet,
>
> Thinks she's ev'rybody's sweet pet.
>
> She slapped my brother,
>
> Fibbed to my mother—
>
> I know what she's going to get.

Mabel snorted indignantly over this injustice to her beloved Bettie and started to rise, but Marjory promptly seized her skirt and dragged her down. Laura, however, saw the movement and was correspondingly elated. It showed in her voice:

> But the worst of the lot is Mabel,
>
> She eats all the pie she's able.
>
> She's round as a ball,
>
> Has no waist at all,
>
> And her manners are bad at the table.

Marjory giggled. She had no thought of being disloyal, but this verse was certainly a close fit.

"You just let me go," muttered Mabel, crimson with resentment and struggling to break away from Marjory's restraining hand. "I'll push her off that post."

"Hush!" said diplomatic Marjory, "perhaps there's more to the song."

But there wasn't. Laura began at the beginning and sang all the verses again, giving particular emphasis to the ones concerning Mabel and Marjory. This, of course, grew decidedly monotonous; the girls got tired of the constant repetition of the silly song long before Laura did. There was something about the song, too, that caught and held their attention. Irresistibly attracted, held by an exasperating fascination, neither girl could help waiting for her own special verse. But while this was going on, Mabel, with a finger in the ear nearest Laura, was industriously scribbling something on a scrap of paper.

As everybody knows, the poetic muse doesn't always work when it is most needed, and Mabel was sadly handicapped at that moment. She was not satisfied with her hasty scrawl but, in the circumstances, it was the best she could do. Suddenly, before Marjory realized what was about to happen, Mabel was shouting back, to an air quite as objectionable as the one Laura was singing:

> There's a very rude girl named Laura,
> Whose ways fill all with horror.
> She's all the things she says we are;
> All know this to their sorrow.

"Yah! yah!" retorted quick-witted Laura. "There isn't a rhyme in your old song. If I couldn't rhyme better 'n that, I'd learn how. Come over and I'll teach you!"

For an instant, Mabel looked decidedly crushed—no poet likes his rhymes disparaged. Laura, noting Mabel's crestfallen attitude, went into gales of mocking laughter and when Mabel looked at Marjory for sympathy Marjory's face was wreathed in smiles. It was too much; Mabel hated to be laughed at.

"I can rhyme," cried Mabel, springing to her feet and giving vent to all her grievances at once. "My table manners are good. I'm not fat. I've got just as much waist as you have."

"You've got more," shrieked delighted Laura.

Faithless Marjory, struck by this indubitable truth, laughed outright.

"You—you can't make Indian-bead chains," sputtered Mabel, trying hard to find something crushing to say. "You can't make pancakes. You can't drive nails."

"Yah," retorted Laura, who was right in her element, "you can't throw straight."

"Neither can you."

"I can! If I could find anything to throw I'd prove it."

Just at this unfortunate moment, a grocery-man arrived at the Milligan house with a basketful of beautiful scarlet tomatoes. In another second, Laura, anxious to prove her ability, had jumped from the fence, seized the basket and, with unerring aim, was delightedly pelting her astonished enemy with the gorgeous fruit. Mabel caught one full in the chest, and as she turned to flee, another landed square in the middle of her light-blue gingham back; Marjory's shoulder stopped a third before the girls retreated to the house, leaving Laura, a picturesque figure on the high post, shouting derisively:

"Proved it, didn't I? Ki! I proved it."

Marjory, pleading that discretion was the better part of valor, begged Mabel to stay indoors; but Mabel, who had received, and undoubtedly deserved, the worst of the encounter, was for instant revenge. Rushing to the kitchen she seized the pan of hard little green apples that Grandma Pike had bequeathed the girls and flew with them to the porch.

Mabel's first shot took Laura by surprise and landed squarely between her shoulders. Mabel was surprised, too, because throwing straight was not one of her accomplishments. She hadn't hoped to do more than frighten her exasperating little neighbor.

Elated by this success, Mabel threw her second apple, which, alas, flew wide of its mark and caught poor unprepared Mr. Milligan, who was coming in at his own gate, just under the jaw, striking in such a fashion that it made the astonished man suddenly bite his tongue.

Nobody likes to bite his tongue. Naturally Mr. Milligan was indignant; indeed, he had every reason to be, for Mabel's conduct was disgraceful and the little apple was very hard. Entirely overlooking the fact that Laura, who had failed to notice her father's untimely arrival, was still vigorously pelting Mabel, who stood as if petrified on the cottage steps and was making no effort to dodge the flying scarlet fruit, Mr. Milligan shouted:

"Look here, you young imps, I'll see that you're turned out of that cottage for this outrage. We've stood just about enough abuse from you. I don't intend to put up with any more of it."

Then, suddenly discovering what Laura, who had turned around in dismay at the sound of her father's voice, was doing, angry Mr. Milligan dragged his suddenly crestfallen daughter from the fence, boxed her ears soundly, and carried what was left of the tomatoes into the house; for that particular basket of fruit had been sent from very far south and express charges had swelled the price of the unseasonable dainty to a very considerable sum.

Marjory, in the cottage kitchen, was alternately scolding and laughing at woebegone Mabel when Jean and Bettie, released from their charge, ran back to Dandelion Cottage. Mabel, crying with indignation, sat on the kitchen stove rubbing her eyes with a pair of grimy fists— Mabel's hands always gathered dust.

"Oh, Mabel! how could you!" groaned Jean, when Marjory had told the afternoon's story. "I'll never dare to leave you here again without some sensible person to look after you. Don't you see you've been almost—yes, quite—as bad as Laura?"

"I don't care," sobbed unrepentant Mabel. "If you'd heard those verses—and—and Marjory laughed at me."

"Couldn't help it," giggled Marjory, who was perched on the corner of the kitchen table.

"But surely," reproached gentle-mannered Jean, "it wasn't necessary to throw things."

"I guess," said Mabel, suddenly sitting up very straight and disclosing a puffy, tear-stained countenance that moved Marjory to fresh giggles, "if you'd felt those icy cold tomatoes go plump in your eye and every place on your very newest dress, you'd have been pretty mad, too. Look at me! I was too surprised to move after I'd hit Mr. Milligan—I never saw him coming at all—and I guess every tomato Laura threw hit me some place."

"Yes," confirmed Marjory, "I'll say that much for Laura. She can certainly throw straighter than any girl I ever knew—she throws just like a boy."

Jean, still worried and disapproving, could not help laughing, for Laura's plump target showed only too good evidence of Laura's skill. Mabel's new light-blue gingham showed a round scarlet spot where each juicy missile had landed; and besides this, there were wide muddy circles where her tears had left highwater marks about each eye.

"But, dear me," said Jean, growing sober again, "think how low-down and horrid it will sound when we tell about it at home. Suppose it should get into the papers! Apples and tomatoes! If boys had done it it would have sounded bad enough, but for girls to do such a thing! Oh, dear, I do wish I'd been here to stop it!"

"To stop the tomatoes, you mean," said Mabel. "You couldn't have stopped anything else, for I just had to do something or burst. I've felt all the week just like something sizzling in a bottle and waiting to have the cork pulled! I'll never be able to do my suffering in silence the way you and Bettie do. Oh, girls, I feel just loads better."

"Well, you may feel better," said irrepressible Marjory, "but you certainly look a lot worse. With those muddy rings on your face you look just like a little owl that isn't very wise."

"Oh, dear," mourned Bettie, "if Miss Blossom had only stayed we wouldn't have had all this trouble with those people."

"No," said Marjory, shrewdly, "Miss Blossom would probably have made Laura over into a very good imitation of an honest citizen. I don't think, though, that even Miss Blossom could make Laura anything more than an imitation, because—well, because she's Laura. It's different with Mabel—"

Mabel looked up expectantly, and Marjory, who was in a teasing mood, continued.

"Yes," said she, encouragingly, "Miss Blossom might have succeeded in making a nice, polite girl out of Mabel if she'd only had time—"

"How much time?" demanded Mabel, with sudden suspicion.

"Oh, about a thousand years," replied Marjory, skipping prudently behind tall Jean.

"Never mind, Mabel," said Bettie, who always sided with the oppressed, slipping a thin arm about Mabel's plump shoulders. "We like you pretty well, anyway, and you've certainly had an awful time."

"Do you think," asked Mabel, with sudden concern, "that Mr. Milligan could get us turned out of the cottage? You know he threatened to."

"No," said Bettie. "The cottage is church property and no one could do anything about it with Mr. Black away because he's the senior warden. Father said only this morning that there was all sorts of church business waiting for him."

"Well," said Mabel, with a sigh of relief, "Mr. Black wouldn't turn us out, so we're perfectly safe. Guess I'll go out on the porch and sing my Milligan song again."

"I guess you won't," said Jean. "There's a very good tub in the Bennett house and I'd advise you to go home and take a bath in it—you look as if you needed two baths and a shampoo. Besides, it's almost supper time."

Laura's version of the story, unfortunately, differed materially from the truth. There was no gainsaying the tomatoes—Mr. Milligan had seen those with his own eyes; but Laura claimed that she had been compelled to use those expensive vegetables as a means of self-defense. According to Laura, whose imagination was as well trained as her arm, she had been the innocent victim of all sorts of persecution at the hands of the four girls. They had called her a thief and had insulted not only her but all the other Milligans. Mabel, she declared, had opened hostilities that afternoon by throwing stones, and poor, abused Laura had only used the tomatoes as a last resort. The apple that struck Mr. Milligan was, she maintained, the very last of about four dozen.

Had the Milligans not been prejudiced, they might easily have learned how far from the truth this assertion was, for the porch of Dandelion Cottage was still bespattered with tomatoes, whereas in the Milligan yard there were no traces of the recent encounter. This, to be sure, was no particular credit to Mabel for there might have been had Mr. Milligan delayed his coming by a very few minutes, since Mabel's pan still contained seven hard little apples and Mabel still longed to use them.

The Milligans, however, were prejudiced. Although Laura was often rude and disagreeable at home, she was the only little girl the Milligans had; in any quarrel with outsiders they naturally sided with their own flesh and blood, and, in spite of the tomatoes, they did so now. In her mother Laura found a staunch champion.

"I won't have those stuck-up little imps there another week," said

Mrs. Milligan. "If you don't see that they're turned out, James, I will."

"They stick out their tongues at me every time they see me," fibbed Laura, whose own tongue was the only one that had been used for sticking-out purposes. "They said Ma was no lady, and—"

"I'm going to complain of them this very night," said Mrs. Milligan, with quick resentment. "I'll show 'em whether I'm a lady or not."

"Who'll you complain to?" asked Laura, hopefully.

"The church warden, of course. These cottages both belong to the church."

"Mr. Black is the girls' best friend," said Laura. "He wouldn't believe anything against them—besides, he's away."

"Mr. Downing isn't," said Mr. Milligan. "I paid him the rent last week. We'll threaten to leave if he doesn't turn them out. He's a sharp businessman and he wouldn't lose the rent of this house for the sake of letting a lot of children use that cottage. I'll see him tomorrow."

"No," said Mrs. Milligan, "just leave the matter to me. I'll talk to Mr. Downing."

"Suit yourself," said Mr. Milligan, glad perhaps to shirk a disagreeable task.

After supper that evening, Mrs. Milligan put on her best hat and went to Mr. Downing's house, which was only about three blocks from her own. The evening was warm and she found Mr. and Mrs. Downing seated on their front porch. Mrs. Milligan accepted their invitation to take a chair and began at once to explain the reason for her visit.

The angry woman's tale lost nothing in the telling; indeed, it was not hard to discover how Laura came by her habit of exaggerating. When Mrs. Milligan went home half an hour later, Mr. Downing was convinced that the church property was in dangerous hands. He couldn't see what Mr. Black had been thinking of to allow careless, impudent children who played with matches, drove nails in the cottage plaster, and insulted innocent neighbors, to occupy Dandelion Cottage.

"Somehow," said Mrs. Downing, when the visitor had departed, "I don't like that woman. She isn't quite a lady."

"Nonsense, my dear," said Mr. Downing. "If only half the things she hints at are true, there would be reason enough for closing the cottage. The place itself doesn't amount to much, I've been told, but a fire started there would damage thousands of dollars' worth of property. Besides, there's the rent from the house those people are in—we don't want to lose that, you know."

"Still, there are always tenants—"

"Not at this time of the year. I'll look into the matter as soon as I can find time."

"Remember," said Mrs. Downing, thinking of Mrs. Milligan's rasping tones, "that there are two sides to every story."

"My dear," said Mr. Downing, complacently, "I shall listen with the strictest impartiality to both sides."

CHAPTER 13.
THE JUNIOR WARDEN

By nine o'clock the next morning, the girls were all at the cottage as usual. Mrs. Mapes had given them materials for a simple cake and Jean and Bettie were in the kitchen making it. Marjory, singing as she worked, was running her Aunty Jane's carpet-sweeper noisily over the parlor rug, while Mabel, whistling an accompaniment to Marjory's song, was dusting the sideboard; at all times the cottage furniture received so much unnecessary dusting that it would not have been at all surprising if it had worn thin in spots.

When the doorbell rang suddenly and sharply, Marjory's tune stopped short, high in air, and Mabel ran to the window.

"It's a man," announced Mabel.

"Mr. Milligan?" asked Marjory, anxiously.

"He's moved so I can't tell."

"Try the other window," urged Marjory, impatiently.

"It doesn't look like Mr. Milligan's legs—I can't see the rest of him. They look neat and—and expensive."

"Probably it's just an agent; they're kind of thick lately. You go to the door and tell him we're just pretend people, while I'm putting the sweeper out of sight."

"Good morning," said Mr. Downing. "Are you—Why! this is a very cozy little place. I had no idea that it was so comfortable. May I come in?"

"Ye-es," returned Mabel, eyeing him doubtfully, "but I think you're probably making a mistake. You see, we're not really-truly people."

"Indeed!" said Mr. Downing, with an amused glance at plump Mabel. "Is it possible you're a ghost?"

"I mean," explained Mabel, "we're just children and this is only a playhouse, not a real one. If you have anything to sell, or are looking for a boarding place, or want to take our census—"

"No," said Mr. Downing, "I don't want either your dollars or your senses. My name is Downing and I'm not selling anything. I called on business. Who is the head of this—this ghostly corporation?"

"It has four," said Mabel. "I'll get the rest."

Bettie and Jean, with grown-up gingham aprons tied about their necks, followed Mabel to the parlor. Mr. Downing had seated himself in one of the chairs and the girls sat facing him in a bright-eyed row on the couch. Their countenances were so eager and expectant that Mr. Downing found it hard to begin.

"I've come in," he said, "to talk over a little matter of business with you. I understand that you've been having trouble with your neighbors—exchanging compliments—"

"No," said honest Mabel, turning crimson, "it was apples and tomatoes. The Milligans are the most troublesome neighbors we've ever had."

"So-o?" said the visitor, raising his eyebrows in genuine surprise. "Why, I understood that it was quite the other way round. I'd like to hear your version of the difficulty."

Jean and Bettie, with occasional assistance from Marjory and much prompting from Mabel, told him all about it. During the recital Mr. Downing's attention seemed to wander, for his eyes took in every detail of the neat sitting-room, strayed to the prettily papered dining-room, and even rested lingeringly upon the one visible corner of the dainty blue bedroom. Bettie had neglected to close the door between the kitchen and the dining-room, which proved unfortunate, because the tiny scrap of butter that Jean had left melting in a very small pan on the kitchen stove, got too hot and with threatening, hissing noises began to give forth clouds of thick, disagreeable smoke. Jean, the first of the girls to notice it, flew to the kitchen, snatched a lid from the stove, and, with a newspaper for a holder, swept the burning butter, pan and all, into the fire. Then the paper in Jean's hand caught fire, and for the instant before she stuffed it into the stove and clapped the lid into place, fierce red flames leaped high.

To the visitor, prepared by Mrs. Milligan for just such doings, it looked for a moment as if all the rear end of the cottage were in flames; but Jean returned to her place on the couch with an air of what looked to Mr. Downing very much like almost criminal unconcern. How was Mr. Downing, who did no cooking, to know that paper placed on a cake-baking fire always flares up in an alarming fashion without doing any real harm? He didn't know, and the incident decided the matter he was turning over in his mind. The girls had found it a little hard to tell their story, for it was plain that their visitor was using his eyes rather than his ears; moreover, they were not at all certain that he had any right to demand the facts in the case. When the story was finished, Mr. Downing looked at the row of interested faces and cleared his throat; but, for some reason, the words he had meant to speak refused to come. He hadn't supposed that the evicting of unsatisfactory tenants would prove such an unpleasant task. The tenants, all at once, seemed part of the house, and the man realized suddenly that the losing of the cottage was likely to prove a severe blow to the four little housekeepers. Perhaps it was disconcerting to see the expression of puzzled anxiety that had crept into Bettie's great brown eyes, into Jean's hazel ones, into Marjory's gray and Mabel's blue ones. At any rate, Mr. Downing decided to be well out of the way when the blow should fall; he realized that it would prove a trying ordeal to face all those young eyes filled with indignation and probably with tears.

"Ah-hum," said Mr. Downing, rising to take his leave. "I'm much obliged to you young ladies. Hum—the number of this house is what, if you please?"

"Number 224," said Bettie, whose mind worked quickly.

"Hum," said Mr. Downing, writing it on the envelope he had taken from his pocket, and moving rather abruptly toward the door, as if desirous to escape as speedily as possible with the knowledge he had gleaned. "Thank you very much. I bid you all good morning."

"Now what in the world did that man want?" demanded Mabel, before the front door had fairly closed. "Do you s'pose he's some kind of a lawyer, or—" and Mabel turned pale at the thought—"a policeman disguised as a—a human being? Do you suppose the Milligans are going to get us arrested for just two apples—and—and a little poetry?"

"More probably," suggested Jean, "he's a burglar. Didn't you notice the way he looked around at everything? I could see that he sort of lost interest after while—as if he had concluded that we hadn't anything worth stealing."

"Nonsense!" said Bettie. "I don't know what he does for a living, but he can't be a burglar. He hasn't lived here very long, but he goes to our church and comes to our house to vestry meetings. Sometimes on warm Sundays when there's nobody else to do it, he passes the plate."

"Well," said Mabel, "I hope he isn't a policeman weekdays."

"It's more likely," said Marjory, "that he does reporting for the papers. The time Aunty Jane was in that railroad accident, a reporter came to our house to interview her, and he asked questions just as that Mr. Downing—was that his name?—did. He took the number of the house, too."

"Oh, mercy!" gasped Mabel, turning suddenly from white to a deep crimson. "If those green apples get into the paper, I'll be too ashamed to live! Oh, girls! Couldn't we stop him—couldn't we—couldn't we pay him something not to?"

"It's probably in by now," said Marjory, teasingly. "They do it by telegraph, you know."

"He couldn't have been a reporter," protested Mabel. "Reporters are always young and very active so they can catch lots of scoons—no, scoots."

"Scoops," corrected Jean.

"Well, scoops. He was kind of slow and a little bit bald-headed on top—I noticed it when he stooped for his hat."

"Well, anyway," comforted Jean, "let's not worry about it. Let's rebuild our fire—of course it's out by now—and finish our cake."

In spite of the cake's turning out much better than anyone could have expected, with so many agitated cooks taking turns stirring it, there was something wrong with the day. The girls were filled with uneasy forebodings and could settle down to nothing. Marjory felt no desire to sing, and even the cake seemed to have lost something of its flavor. Moreover, when they had stood for a moment on their doorstep to see the new steam road-roller go puffing by, Laura had tossed her head triumphantly and shouted taunt-ingly: "I know something I shan't tell!" After that, the girls could not help wondering if Laura really did know something—some dreadful thing that concerned them vitally and was likely to burst upon them at any moment.

For the first time in the history of their housekeeping, they could find nothing that they really wanted to do. During the afternoon they had several little disagreements with each other. Mild Jean spoke sharply to Marjory, and even sweet-tempered Bettie was drawn into a lively dis-pute with Mabel. Moreover, all three of the older girls were inclined to blame Mabel for her fracas with the Milligans; and the culprit, ashamed one moment and defiant the next, was in a most unhappy frame of mind. Altogether, the day was a failure and the four friends parted coldly at least an hour before the usual time.

CHAPTER 14.
AN UNEXPECTED LETTER

The next morning, Jean, with three large bananas as a peace offer-ing, was the first to arrive at Dandelion Cottage. Jean, a wise young person for her years, had decided that a little hard work would clear the atmosphere, so, finding no one else in the house, she made a fire in the stove, put on the kettle, put up the leaf of the kitchen table, and began to take all the dishes from the pantry shelves. Dishwashing in the cottage was always far more enjoyable than this despised occupation usually is elsewhere, owing to the astonishing assortment of crockery the girls had accumulated. No two of the dishes—with the exception of a pair of plates bearing life-sized portraits of "The frog that would a-wooing go, whether his mother would let him or no"—bore the same pattern. There was a bewildering diversity, too, in the sizes and shapes of the cups and saucers, and an alarming variety in the matter of color. But, as the girls had declared gleefully a dozen times or more, it would be possible to set the table for seven courses when the time should come for Mr. Black's and Mrs. Crane's dinner party, because so many of the things almost matched if they didn't quite. Jean was thinking of this as she lifted the dishes from the shelf to the table, and lovingly arranged them in pairs, the pink sugar bowl beside the blue cream-pitcher, the yellow coffee cup beside the dull red Japanese tea cup, and the "Love-the-Giver" mug beside the "For my Little Friend" oatmeal bowl. She had just taken down the big, dusty, cracked pitcher that matched nothing else—which perhaps was the reason that it had remained high on the shelf since the day Mabel had used it for her lemonade—when the doorbell rang.

Hastily wiping her dusty hands, Jean ran to the door. No one was there, but the postman was climbing the steps of the next house, so Jean slipped her fingers expectantly into the little, rusty iron letter-box. Perhaps there was something from Miss Blossom, who sometimes showed that she had not forgotten her little landladies.

Sure enough, there was a large white letter, not from Miss Blossom to be sure, but from somebody. To the young cottagers, letters were always joyous happenings; they had no debts, consequently they were unacquainted with bills. With this auspicious beginning, for of course the coming of a totally unexpected letter was an auspicious beginning, it was surely going to be a cheerful, perhaps even a delightful, day. Jean hummed happily as she laid the unopened letter on the dining-room table, for of course a letter somewhat oddly addressed to "The Four Young Ladies at 224 Fremont Street, City," could be opened only when all four were present. When Marjory and Bettie came in, they fell upon the letter and examined every portion of the envelope, but neither girl could imagine who had sent it. It was impossible to wait for Mabel, who was always late, so Bettie obligingly ran to get her. Even so there was still a considerable wait while Mabel laced her shoes; but presently Bettie returned, with Mabel, still nibbling very-much-buttered toast, at her heels.

"You open it, Jean," panted Bettie. "You can read writing better than we can."

"Hurry," urged Mabel, who could keep other persons waiting much more easily than she herself could wait.

"Here's a fork to open it with," said Marjory. "I can't find the scissors. Hurry up; maybe it's a party and we'll have to R. S. V. P. right away."

"Oh, goody! If it is," squealed Mabel, "I can wear my new tan Oxfords."

"It's from Yours respectably—no, Yours regretfully, John W. Downing," announced Jean. "The man that was here yesterday, you know."

"Read it, read it," pleaded the others, crowding so close that Jean had to lift the letter above their heads in order to see it at all. "Do hurry up, we're crazy to hear it."

"My Dear Young Ladies," read Jean in a voice that started bravely but grew fainter with every line. "It is with sincere regret that I write to inform you that it no longer suits the convenience of the vestrymen to have you occupy the church cottage on Fremont Street. It is to be rented as soon as a few necessary repairs can be made, and in the meantime you will oblige us greatly by moving out at once. Please deliver the key at your earliest convenience to me at either my house or this office.

"Yours regretfully,

"John W. Downing."

For as much as two minutes no one said a word. Jean had laid the open letter on the table. Marjory and Bettie with their arms tightly locked, as if both felt the need of support, reread the closely written page in silence. When they reached the end, they pushed it toward Mabel.

"What does it mean in plain English?" asked Mabel, hoping that both her eyes and her ears had deceived her.

"That somebody else is to have the cottage," said Jean, "and that in the meantime we're to move."

"In the meantime!" blurted Mabel, with swift wrath. "I should say it was the meantime—the very meanest time anybody ever heard of.

I'd just like to know what right 'Yours-respectably-John-W.-Downing' has to turn us out of our own house. I guess we paid our rent—I guess there's blisters on me yet—I guess I dug dandelions—I guess I—"

But here Mabel's indignation turned to grief, and with one of her very best howls and a torrent of tears she buried her face in Jean's apron.

"Bettie," asked Jean with her arms about Mabel, "do you think it would do any good to ask your father about it? He's the minister, you know, and he might explain to Mr. Downing that we were promised the cottage for all summer."

"Papa went away this morning and won't be home for ten days. He has exchanged with somebody for the next two Sundays."

"My pa-pa-papa's away, too," sobbed Mabel, "or he'd tell that vile Mr. Downing that it was all the Mill-ill-igans' fault. They're the folks that ought to be turned out, and I just wuh-wuh-wish they—they had been."

"Why wouldn't it be a good idea," suggested Marjory, "for us all to go down to Mr. Downing's office and tell him all about it? You see, he hasn't lived here very long and perhaps he doesn't understand that we have paid our rent for all summer."

"Yes," assented Jean, "that would probably be the best thing to do. He won't mind having us go to the office because he told us to take the key there. But where is his office?"

"I know," said Bettie. "Here's the address on the letter, and the dentist I go to is right near there, so I can find it easily."

"Then let's start right away," cried eager Mabel, uncovering a disheveled head and a tear-stained countenance. "Don't let's lose a minute."

"Mercy, no," said Jean, taking Mabel by the shoulders and pushing her before her to the blue-room mirror. "Do you think you can go any place looking like that? Do you think you look like a desirable tenant? We've all got to be just as clean and neat as we can be. We've got to impress him with our—our ladylikeness."

"I'll braid Mabel's hair," offered Bettie, "if Marjory will run around the block and get all our hats. I'm wearing Dick's straw one with the blue ribbon just now, Marjory. You'll find it some place in our front hall if Tommy hasn't got it on."

"Bring mine, too," said Jean; "it's in my room."

"I don't know where mine is," said Mabel, "but if you can't find it you'd better wear your Sunday one and lend me your everyday one."

"I don't see myself lending you any more hats," said Marjory, who had, like the other girls, brightened at the prospect of going to Mr. Downing's. "I haven't forgotten how you left the last one outdoors all night in the rain, and how it looked afterwards, when Aunty Jane made me wear it to punish me for my carelessness. You'll go in your own hat or none."

"Well," said Mabel, meekly, "I guess you'll probably find it in my room under the bed, if it isn't in the parlor behind the sofa."

"Now, remember," said Jean, who was retying the bow on Bettie's hair, "we're all to be polite, whatever happens, for we mustn't let Mr. Downing think we're anything like the Milligans. If he won't let us have the cottage when he knows about the rent's being paid—though I'm almost sure he will let us keep it—why, we'll just have to give it up and not let him see that we care."

"I'll be good," promised Bettie.

"You needn't be afraid of me," said Mabel. "I wouldn't humble myself to speak to such a despisable man."

CHAPTER 15.
AN OBDURATE LANDLORD

Twenty minutes later when Mr. Downing roared "Come in" in the terrifying voice he usually reserved for agents and other unexpected or unwelcome visitors, he was plainly very much surprised to see four pale girls with shocked, reproachful eyes file in and come to an embarrassed standstill just inside the office door, which closed of its own accord and left them imprisoned with the enemy. They waited quietly.

"Oh, good morning," said he, in a much milder tone, as he swung about in his revolving chair. "What can I do for you? Have you brought the key so soon?"

"We came," said Jean, propelled suddenly forward by a vigorous push from the rear, "to see you about Dandelion Cottage. We think you've made a mistake."

"Indeed!" said Mr. Downing, who did not at any time like to be considered mistaken. "Suppose you explain."

So sweet-voiced Jean explained all about digging the dandelions to pay the rent, about Mr. Black's giving them the key at the end of the week, and about all the lovely times they had had and were still hoping to have in their precious cottage before giving it up for the winter.

Mr. Downing, personally, did not like Mr. Black. He had a poor opinion of the older man's business ability, and perhaps a somewhat exalted opinion of his own. He considered Mr. Black old-fashioned and far too easy-going. He felt that parish affairs were more likely to flourish in the hands of a younger, shrewder, and more modern person, and he had an idea that he was that person. At any rate, now that Mr. Black was out of town, Mr. Downing was glad of an opportunity to display his own superior shrewdness. He would show the vestry a thing or two, and incidentally increase the parish income, which as everybody knew stood greatly in need of increasing. He had no patience with slipshod methods. He was truly sorry when business matters compelled him to appear hard-hearted; but to him it seemed little short of absurd for a man of Mr. Black's years to waste on four small girls a cottage that might be bringing in a comfortable sum every month in the year.

"Now that's a very pretty little story," said Mr. Downing, when Jean had finished. "But, you see, you've already had the cottage more than long enough to pay you for pulling those few weeds."

"Few!" exclaimed Mabel, in indignant protest and forgetting her promise of silence. "Few! Why, there were billions of 'em. If we'd been paid two cents a hundred for them, we'd all be rich. Mr. Black promised us we could have that cottage for all summer and our rent hasn't half perspired yet."

"She means expired," explained Marjory, "but she's right for once. Mr. Black did say we could stay there all summer, and it isn't quite August yet, you know."

"Hum," said Mr. Downing. "Nobody said anything to me about any such arrangement, and I'm keeping the books. I don't know what Mr. Black could have been thinking of if he made any such foolish promise as that. Of course it's not binding. Why, that cottage ought to be renting for ten or twelve dollars a month!"

"But the plaster's very bad," pleaded Bettie, eagerly, "and the roof leaks in every room in the house but one, and something's the matter underneath so it's too cold for folks to live in during the winter. It was vacant for a long time before we had it."

"It looked very comfortable to me," said Mr. Downing, who had lived in the town for only a few months and neither knew nor suspected the real condition of the house. "I'm afraid your arrangement with Mr. Black doesn't hold good. Mr. Morgan and I think it best to have the house vacated at once. You see, we're in danger of losing the rent from the next house, because the Milligans have threatened to move out if you don't."

"If—if seven dollars and a half would do you any good," said Mabel, "and if you're mean enough to take all the money we've got in this world—"

"I'm not," said Mr. Downing. "I'm only reasonable, and I want you to be reasonable too. You must look at this thing from a business standpoint. You see, the rent from those two houses should bring in twenty-five dollars a month, which isn't more than a sufficient return for the money invested. The taxes—"

"A note for you, Mr. Downing," said a boy, who had quietly opened the office door.

"Why," said Mr. Downing, when he had read the note, "this is really quite a remarkable coincidence. This communication is from Mr. Milligan, who has found a desirable tenant for the cottage he is now in, and wishes, himself, to occupy the cottage you are going to vacate. Very clever idea on Mr. Milligan's part. This will save him five dollars a month and is a most convenient arrangement all around. He wishes to move in at once."

"Mr. Milligan!" gasped three of the astonished girls.

"Those Milligans in our house!" cried Mabel. "Well, isn't that the worst!"

"You see," said Mr. Downing, "it is really necessary for you to move at once. I think you had better begin without further loss of time. Good morning, good morning, all of you, and please believe me, I'm sorry about this, but it can't be helped."

"I hope," said Mabel, summoning all her dignity for a parting shot, "that you'll never live long enough to regret this—this outrage. There are seven rolls of paper on the walls of that cottage that belong to us, and we expect to be paid for every one of them."

"How much?" asked Mr. Downing, suppressing a smile, for Mabel was never more amusing than when she was very angry.

"Five cents a roll—thirty-five cents altogether."

Mr. Downing gravely reached into his trousers pocket, fished up a handful of loose change, scrupulously counted out three dimes and a nickel, and handed them to Mabel, who, with averted eyes and chin held unnecessarily high, accepted the price of the Blossom wall paper haughtily, and, following the others, stalked from the office.

The unhappy girls could not trust themselves to talk as they hastened homeward. They held hands tightly, walking four abreast along the quiet street, and barely managed to keep the tears back and the rapidly swelling lumps in their little throats successfully swallowed until Jean's trembling fingers had unlocked the cottage door.

Then, with one accord, they rushed pell-mell for the blue-room bed, hurled themselves upon its excelsior pillows, and burst into tears. Jean and Bettie cried silently but bitterly; Marjory wept audibly, with long, shuddering sobs; but Mabel simply bawled. Mabel always did her crying on the excellent principle that, if a thing were worth doing at all, it was worth doing well. She was doing it so well on this occasion that Jean, who seldom cried and whose puffed, scarlet eyelids contrasted oddly and rather pathetically with her colorless cheeks, presently sat up to remonstrate.

"Mabel!" she said, slipping an arm about the chief mourner, "do you want the Milligans to hear you? We're on their side of the house, you know."

Jean couldn't have used a better argument. Mabel stopped short in the middle of one of her very best howls, sat up, and shook her head vigorously.

"Well, I just guess I don't," said she. "I'd die first!"

"I thought so," said Jean, with just a faint glimmer of a smile. "We mustn't let those people guess how awfully we care. Go bathe your eyes, Mabel—there must be a little warm water in the tea kettle."

Then the comforter turned to Bettie, and made the appeal that was most likely to reach that always-ready-to-help young person.

"Come, Bettie dear, you've cried long enough. We must get to work, for we've a tremendous lot to do. Don't you suppose that, if we had all the things packed in baskets or bundles, we could get a few of your brothers to help us move out after dark? I just can't let those Milligans gloat over us while we go back and forth with things."

Bettie's only response was a sob.

"Where in the world can we put the things?" asked Marjory, sitting up suddenly and displaying a blotched and swollen countenance very unlike her usual fair, rose-tinted face. "Of course we can each take our dolls and books home, but our furniture—"

"I'm going to ask Mother if we can't store it upstairs in our barn. I'm sure she'll let us."

"Oh, I wish Mr. Black were here. It doesn't seem possible we've really got to move. There must be some way out of it. Oh, Bettie, couldn't we write to Mr. Black?"

"It would take too-oo-oo long," sobbed Bettie, sitting up and mopping her eyes with the muslin window curtain, which she could easily reach from the foot of the bed. "He's way off in Washington. Oh, dear—

oh, dear—oh, dear!"

"Why couldn't we telegraph?" demanded Marjory, with whom hope died hard. "Telegrams go pretty fast, don't they?"

"They cost terribly," said Bettie. "They're almost as expensive as express packages. Still, we might find out what it costs."

"I dow the telegraph-mad," wheezed Mabel from the wash-basin. "I'll go hobe ad telephode hib ad ask what it costs—I've heard by father give hib bessages lots of tibes. Oh, by, by dose is all stuffed up."

"Try a handkerchief," suggested Jean. "Go ask, if you want to; it won't do any harm, nor probably any good."

Mabel ran home, taking care to keep her back turned toward the Milligan house. During her brief absence, the girls bathed their eyes and made sundry other futile attempts to do away with all outward signs of grief.

"He says," cried Mabel, bursting in excitedly, "that sixty cents is the regular price in the daytime, but it's forty cents for a night message. It seems kind of mean to wake folks up in the middle of the night just to save twenty cents, doesn't it?"

"Yes," said Bettie. "I couldn't be impolite enough to do that to anybody I like as well as I like Mr. Black. If we haven't money enough to send a daytime message, we mustn't send any."

"Well, we haven't," said Jean. "We've only thirty-five cents."

"And we wouldn't have had that," said Mabel, "if I hadn't remembered that wall paper just in the nick of time."

Strangely enough, not one of the girls thought of the money in the bank. Perhaps it did not occur to them that it would be possible to remove any portion of their precious seven dollars and a half without withdrawing it all; they knew little of business matters. Nor did they think of appealing to their parents for aid at this crisis. Indeed, they were all too dazed by the suddenness and tremendousness of the blow to think very clearly about anything. The sum needed seemed a large one to the girls, who habitually bought a cent's worth of candy at a time from the generous proprietor of the little corner shop. Mabel, the only one with an allowance, was, to her father's way of thinking, a hopeless little spendthrift, already deeply plunged in debt by her unpaid fines for lateness to meals.

The Tucker income did not go round even for the grown-ups, so of course there were few pennies for the Tucker children. Marjory's Aunty Jane had ideas of her own on the subject of spending-money for little girls—Marjory did not suspect that the good but rather austere woman made a weekly pilgrimage to the bank for the purpose of religiously depositing a small sum in her niece's name; and, if she had known it, Marjory would probably have been improvident enough to prefer spot cash in smaller amounts. Only that morning tender-hearted Jean had heard patient Mrs. Mapes lamenting because butter had gone up two cents a pound and because all the bills had seemed larger than those of the preceding month—Jean always took the family bills very much to heart.

The girls sorrowfully concluded that there was nothing left for them to do but to obey Mr. Downing. They had looked forward with dread to giving up the cottage when winter should come, but the idea of losing it in midsummer was a thousand times worse.

"We'll just have to give it up," said grieved little Bettie. "There's nothing else we can do, with Mr. Black away. When I go home tonight I'll write to him and apologize for not being able to keep our promise about the dinner party. That's the hardest thing of all to give up."

"But you don't know his address," objected Jean.

"Yes, I do, because Father wrote to him about some church business this morning, before going away, and gave Dick the letter to mail. Of course Dick forgot all about it and left it on the hall mantelpiece. It's probably there yet, for I'm the only person that ever remembers to mail Father's letters—he forgets them himself most of the time."

"Now let's get to work," said Jean. "Since we have to move let's pretend we really want to. I've always thought it must be quite exciting to really truly move. You see, we must get it over before the Milligans guess that we've begun, and there isn't any too much time left. I'll begin to take down the things in the parlor and tie them up in the bedclothes. We'll leave all the curtains until the last so that no one will know what we're doing."

"I'll help you," said Bettie.

"Mabel and I might be packing the dishes," said Marjory. "It will be easier to do it while we have the table left to work on. Come along, Mabel."

Mabel followed obediently. When the forlorn pair reached the kitchen, Marjory announced her intention of exploring the little shed for empty baskets, leaving Mabel to stack the cups and plates in compact piles. Mabel, without knowing just why she did it, picked up her old friend, the cracked lemonade-pitcher and gave it a little shake. Something rattled. Mabel, always an inquisitive young person, thrust her fingers into the dusty depths to bring up a piece of money—two pieces—three pieces—four pieces.

"Oh," she gasped, "it's my lemonade money! Oh, what a lucky omen! Girls!"

The next instant Mabel clapped a plump, dusty hand over her own lips to keep them from announcing the discovery, and then, stealthily concealing the twenty cents in the pocket that still contained the wallpaper money, she stole quickly through the cottage and ran to her own home.

CHAPTER 16.
MABEL PLANS A SURPRISE

The girls were indignant later when they discovered Mabel's appar-
ent desertion. It was precisely like Mabel, they said, to shirk when
there was anything unpleasant to be done. For once, however, they were
wronging Mabel—poor, self-sacrificing Mabel, who with fifty-five cents
at her disposal was planning a beautiful surprise for her unappreciative
cottage-mates. The girls might have known that nothing short of an
ambitious project for saving the cottage from the Milligans would have
kept the child away when so much was going on. For Mabel was at that
very moment doing what was for her the hardest kind of work; all alone
in her own room at home she was laboriously composing a telegram.

She had never sent a telegram, nor had she even read one. She could
not consult her mother because Mrs. Bennett had inconsiderately gone
down town to do her marketing. Dr. Bennett, however, was a very
busy man and sometimes received a number of important messages in
one day. Mabel felt that the occasion justified her studying several late
specimens which she resurrected from the waste-paper basket under
her father's desk. These, however, proved rather unsatisfactory models
since none of them seemed to exactly fit the existing emergency. Most

of them, indeed, were in cipher.

"I suppose," said Mabel, nibbling her penholder thoughtfully, "they make 'em short so they'll fit these little sheets of yellow paper, but there's lots more space they might use if they didn't leave such wide margins. I'll write small so I can say all I want to, but, dear me, I can't think of a thing to say."

It took a long time, but the message was finished at last. With a deep sigh of satisfaction, Mabel folded it neatly and put it into an envelope which she carefully sealed. Then, putting on her hat, and taking the telegram with her, she ran to Bettie's home and opened the door—none of the four girls were required to ring each other's doorbells. There, sure enough, was the letter waiting to be mailed to Mr. Black. Mabel, who had thought to bring a pencil, copied the address in her big, vertical handwriting, and without further ado ran with it to her friend, the telegraph operator, whose office was just around the corner. All the distances in the little town were short, and Mabel had frequently been sent to the place with messages written by her father, so she did not feel the need of asking permission.

The clerk opened the envelope—Mabel considered this decidedly rude of him—and proceeded to read the message. It took him a long time. Then he looked from Mabel's flushed cheeks and eager eyes to the little collection of nickels and dimes she had placed on the counter. Mabel wondered why the young man chewed the ends of his sandy mustache so vigorously. Perhaps he was amused at something; she looked about the little office to see what it could be that pleased him so greatly, but there seemed to be nothing to excite mirth. She decided that he was either a very cheerful young man naturally, or else he was feeling joyful because the clock said that it was nearly time for luncheon.

"It'll be all right, Miss Mabel," said he at last. "It's a pretty good fifty-five cents' worth; but I guess Mr. Black won't object to that. I hope you'll always come to me when you have messages to send."

"I won't if you go and read them all," said Mabel, at which her friend looked even more cheerful than he had before.

Ten minutes later Mabel, mumbling something about having had an errand to attend to, presented herself at the cottage. Beyond a few meekly received reproaches from Marjory, no one said anything about the unexplained absence. Indeed, they were all too busy and too preoccupied to care, the greater grief of losing the cottage having swallowed up all lesser concerns.

At a less trying time the girls would have discovered within ten minutes that Mabel was suffering from a suppressed secret; but everything was changed now. Although Mabel fairly bristled with importance and gave out sundry very broad hints, no one paid the slightest attention. Gradually, in the stress of packing, the matter of the telegram faded from Mabel's short memory, for preparing to move proved a most exciting operation, and also a harrowing one. Every few moments somebody would say: "Our last day," and then the other three would fall to weeping on anything that happened to come handy. Of course the packing had stirred up considerable dust; this, mingled with tears, added much to the forlornness of the cottagers' appearance when they went home at noon with their news.

The parents and Aunty Jane said it was a shame, but all agreed that there was nothing to be done. All were sorry to have the girls deprived of the cottage, for the mothers had certainly found it a relief to have their little daughters' leisure hours so safely and happily occupied. Mabel's mother was especially sorry.

Never was moving more melancholy nor house more forlorn when the moving, done after dark with great caution, and mostly through the dining-room window on the side of the house farthest from the Milligans, was finally accomplished. The Tucker boys had been only too delighted to help. By bedtime the cottage was empty of everything but the curtains on the Milligan side of the house. An hour later the tired girls were asleep; but under each pillow there was a handkerchief rolled in a tight, grimy little ball and soaked with tears.

In the morning, the girls returned for a last look, and for the remaining curtains. Dandelion Cottage, stripped of its furniture and without its pictures, showed its age and all its infirmities. Great patches of plaster and wall paper were missing, for the gay posters had covered a multitude of defects. The indignant Tucker boys had disobeyed Bettie and had removed not only the tin they had put on the leaking roof, but the steps they had built at the back door, the drain they had found it necessary to place under the kitchen sink, and the bricks with which they had propped the tottering chimneys.

Before the day was over, the tenants whom the Milligans had found for their own house were clamoring to move in, so the Milligans took possession of the cottage late that afternoon, getting the key from Mr. Downing, into whose keeping the girls had silently delivered it that morning. To do Mr. Downing justice, nothing had ever hurt him quite as much as did the dignified silence of the three pale girls who waited for a moment in the doorway, while equally pallid Jean went quietly forward to lay the key on his desk. He realized suddenly that not one of them could have spoken a word without bursting into tears; and for the rest of that day he hated himself most heartily.

CHAPTER 17.
SEVERAL SURPRISES
TAKE EFFECT

Mr. Black opened the door of his hotel apartment in Washington one sultry noon in response to a vigorous, prolonged rapping from without. The bellboy handed him a telegram. When Mr. Black had read the long message he smiled and frowned, but cheerfully paid the three dollars and forty-one cents additional charges that the messenger demanded.

It was Mabel's message; the clerk had transmitted it faithfully, even to the two misspelled words that had proved too much for the excited little writer. If the receiving clerk had not considerately tucked in a few periods for the sake of clearness, there would have been no punctuation marks, because, as everybody knows, very few telegrams are punctuated; but Mabel, of course, had not taken that into consideration. It was quite the longest message and certainly the most amusing one that Mr. Black had ever received. It read:

"Dear Mr. Black,

"We are well but terribly unhappy for the worst has happened. Cant you come to the reskew as they say in books for we are really in great trouble because the Milligans a very unpolite and untruthful family next door want dandelion cottage for themselves the pigs and Mr. Downing says we must move out at once and return the key our own darling key that you gave us. We are moving out now and crying so hard we can hardly write. I mean myself. Is Mr. Downing the boss of the whole church. Cant you tell him we truly paid the rent for all summer by digging dandelions. He does not believe us. We are too sad to write any more with love from your little friends

"Jean Marjory Bettie and I.

"P. S. How about your dinner party if we lose the cottage?"

Mr. Black read and reread the typewritten yellow sheet a great many times; sometimes he frowned, sometimes he chuckled; the postscript seemed to please him particularly, for whenever he reached that point his deep-set eyes twinkled merrily. Presently he propped the dispatch against the wall at the back of his table and sat down in front of it to write a reply. He wrote several messages, some long, some short; then he tore them all up—they seemed inadequate compared with Mabel's.

"That man Downing," said he, dropping the scraps into the wastebasket, "means well, but he muddles every pie he puts his finger in. Probably if I wire him he'll botch things worse than ever. Dear me, it is too bad for those nice children to lose any part of their precious stay in that cottage, now, for of course they'll have to give it up when cold weather comes. If I can wind my business up today there isn't any good reason why I can't go straight through without stopping in Chicago. It's time I was home, anyway; it's pretty warm here for a man that likes a cold climate."

Meanwhile, things were happening in Mr. Black's own town.

It was a dark, threatening day when the Milligans, delighted at the success of their efforts to dislodge its rightful tenants, hurriedly moved into Dandelion Cottage; but, dark though it was, Mrs. Milligan soon began to find her new possession full of unsuspected blemishes. Now that the pictures were down and the rugs were up, she discovered the badly broken plaster, the tattered condition of the wall paper, the leaking drain, and the clumsily mended rat-holes. She found, too, that she had made a grievous mistake in her calculations. She had supposed that the tiny pantry was a third bedroom; with its neat muslin curtains, it certainly looked like one when viewed from the outside; and crafty Laura, intensely desirous of seeing the enemy ousted from the cottage at any price, had not considered it necessary to enlighten her mother.

"My goodness!" exclaimed Mrs. Milligan, a thin woman with a shrewish countenance now much streaked with dust. "I thought you said there was a fine cellar under this house? It's barely three feet deep, and there's no stairs and no floor. It's full of old rubbish."

"I never was down there," admitted Laura, dropping a dishpanful of cooking utensils with a crash and hastily making for safe quarters behind a mountain of Milligan furniture, "but I've often seen the trap door."

"It hasn't been opened for years. And where's the nice big closet you said opened off the bedroom? There isn't a decent closet in this house. I don't see what possessed you—"

"It serves you right," said Mr. Milligan, unsympathetically. "You wouldn't wait for anything, but had to rush right in. I told you you'd better take your time about it, but no—"

"You know very well, James Milligan," snapped the irate lady, "that the Knapps wouldn't have taken our house if they couldn't have had it at once."

"Well, I don't know," growled Mr. Milligan, scowling crossly at the constantly growing heaps of incongruously mixed household goods, "where in Sam Hill you're going to put all that stuff. There isn't room for a cat to turn around, and the place ain't fit to live in, anyway."

Bad as things looked, even Mr. Milligan did not guess that first busy day how hopelessly out of repair the cottage really was; but he was soon to find out.

The summer had been an unusually dry one; so dry that the girls had been obliged to carry many pails of water to their garden every evening. The moving-day had been cloudy—out of sympathy, perhaps, for the little cottagers. That night it rained, the first long, steady downpour in weeks. This proved no gentle shower, but a fierce, robust, pelting flood. Seemingly a discriminating rain, too, choosing carefully between the just and the unjust, for most of it fell upon the Milligans. With the sole exception of the dining-room, every room in the house leaked like a sieve.

The tired, disgusted Milligans, drenched in their beds, leaped hastily from their shower baths to look about, by candlelight, for shelter. Mr. Milligan spread a mattress, driest side up, on the dining-room floor, and the unfortunate family spent the rest of the night huddled in an uncomfortable heap in the one dry spot the house afforded.

Very early the next morning they sent post-haste for Mr. Downing.

Mr. Downing, who hated to be disturbed before eight, arrived at ten o'clock; and, with an expert carpenter, made a thorough examination of the house, which the rain had certainly not improved.

"It will take three hundred—possibly four hundred dollars," said the carpenter, who had been making a great many figures in a worn little note-book, "to make this place habitable. It needs a new roof, new chimneys, new floors, a new foundation, new plumbing, new plaster—in short, just about everything except the four outside walls. Then there are no lights and no heating plant, which of course would be extra. It's probably one of the oldest houses in town. What's it renting for?"

"Ten dollars a month."

"It isn't worth it. Half that money would be a high price. Even if it were placed in good repair it would be six years at least before you could expect to get the money expended on repairs back in rent. The only thing to do is to tear it down and build a larger and more modern house that will bring a better rent, for there's no money in a ten-dollar house on a lot of this size—the taxes eat all the profits."

"Well," said Mr. Downing, "this house certainly looked far more com-

WE'RE THE PEOPLE THAT HAVE BEEN DECEIVED," SAID MRS.
MILLIGAN.

fortable when I saw it the other day than it does now. Those children must have had the defects very well concealed. They deceived me completely."

"They deceived us all," said Mrs. Milligan, resentfully. "Half of our furniture is ruined. Look at that sofa!"

Mr. Downing looked. The drenched old-gold plush sofa certainly looked very much like a half-drowned Jersey calf.

"Of course," continued Mrs. Milligan, sharply, "we expect to have our losses made good. Then we've had all our trouble for nothing, too. Of course we can't stay here—the place isn't fit for pigs. I suppose the best thing we can do is to move right back into our own house."

"Ye-es," said Mr. Milligan, overlooking the fact that Mrs. Milligan had inadvertently called her family pigs, "it certainly looks like the best thing to do. I'll go and tell the Knapps that they'll have to move out at once—we can't spend another night under this roof."

The Knapps, however, proved disobliging and flatly declined to move a second time. The Milligans had begged them to take the house off their hands, and they had signed a contract. Moreover, it was just the kind of house the Knapps had long been looking for, and now that they were moved, more than half settled, and altogether satisfied with their part of the bargain, they politely but firmly announced their intention of staying where they were until the lease should expire.

There was nothing the former tenants could do about it. They were homeless and quite as helpless as the four little girls had been in similar circumstances; and they made a far greater fuss about it. By this they gained, however, nothing but the disapproval of everybody concerned; so, finally, the Milligans, disgusted with Dandelion Cottage, with Mr. Downing, and for once even a little bit with themselves, dejectedly hunted up a new home in a far less pleasant neighborhood, and moved hurriedly out of Dandelion Cottage—and, except for the memories they left behind them, out of the story.

CHAPTER 18.
A HURRIED RETREAT

The girls, of course, had been barred out while all these exciting latest events were taking place in their dear cottage; but Marjory, who lived next door to it, had seen something of the Milligans' hasty exit and had guessed at part of the truth. Mrs. Knapp, who seemed a pleasant, likable little woman, in spite of her unwillingness to accommodate her new landlord, unknowingly confirmed their suspicions when she told her friend Mrs. Crane about it; for Mrs. Crane, in her turn, told the news to the four little housekeepers the next morning as they sat homeless and forlorn on her doorstep. It was always Mrs. Crane to whom the Dandelion Cottagers turned whenever they were in need of consolation and, as in this case, consolation was usually forthcoming.

The girls, in their excitement at hearing the news about their late possession, did not notice that sympathetic Mrs. Crane looked tired and worried as she sat, in the big red rocking chair on her porch, peeling potatoes.

"Oh!" squealed Mabel, from the broad arm of Mrs. Crane's chair, "I'm glad! I'm glad! I'm glad!"

"I can't help being a little bit glad, too," said fair-minded Jean. "I suppose it wasn't very pleasant for the Milligans, but I guess they deserved all they got."

"They deserved a great deal more," said Marjory, resentfully. "Think of these last awful days!"

"If they'd had much more," said Mrs. Crane, "they'd have been drowned. Why, children! the place was just flooded."

"I'm ashamed to tell of it," said Bettie, "but I'm awfully afraid that our boys took off part of the pieces of tin that they nailed on the roof last spring. I heard them doing something up there the night we moved; but Bob only grinned when I asked him about it."

"Good for the boys!" cried Marjory, gleefully. "I wouldn't be unlady-like enough to set traps for the Milligans myself, but I can't help feeling glad that somebody else did."

"It was Bob's own tin," giggled delighted Mabel, almost tumbling into Mrs. Crane's potato pan in her joy. "I guess he had a right to take it home if he wanted to."

"Anyway," said Jean, from her perch on the porch railing, "I'm glad they're gone."

"But it doesn't do us any good," sighed Bettie. "And the summer's just flying."

"Yes, it does," insisted Jean. "We can stand having the cottage empty—we can pretend, you know, that it's an enchanted castle that can be opened only by a certain magic key that—"

"Somebody's baby has swallowed," shrieked Mabel, the matter-of-fact.

"Mercy no, goosie," said Marjory. "She means a magic word that nobody can remember."

"That's it," said Jean. "Of course we couldn't do even that with the cottage full of Milligans."

"No," assented Marjory, "the most active imagination would refuse to activate—"

"To what?" gasped Mabel.

"To work," explained Marjory.

"I should say so," agreed Mabel, again threatening the potatoes. "It was just as much as I could do to come over here this morning to breathe the same air with that cottage with those folks in it staring me in the face, but now—"

"After all," sighed Bettie, sorrowfully, from the other arm of Mrs. Crane's big chair, "having the Milligans out of the cottage doesn't make much difference, as long as we're out, too. Oh, I did love that little house so. I just hated to think of cold weather coming to drive us out; but I never dreamed of anything so dreadful as having to leave it right in this lovely warm weather."

"If Mr. Black had stayed in town," said Mabel, feelingly, "we'd be dusting that darling cottage this very minute."

Mrs. Crane sniffed in the odd way she always did whenever Mr. Black's name was mentioned. This scornful sniff, accompanying Mrs. Crane's evident disapproval of their dearest friend, was the only thing that the girls disliked about Mrs. Crane.

"I know you'd like Mr. Black if you only knew him," said Bettie, earnestly. "In some ways you're a good deal like him. You're both the same color, your eyebrows turn up the same way at the outside corners, and you both like us. Mr. Black has a beautiful soul."

"Indeed," said Mrs. Crane. "And haven't I a beautiful soul too?"

"Why, of course," said Bettie, leaning down to rub her cheek against Mrs. Crane's. "I meant both of you. We like you both just the same."

"Only it's different," explained Jean. "Mr. Black doesn't need us, and sometimes you do. We like to do things for you."

"I'm glad of that," said Mrs. Crane, "for I need you this very minute. But don't you be too sure about his not needing you as well. He must lead a pretty lonely life, because it's years since his wife died. I never heard of anybody else liking her, but I guess he did. He's one of the faithful kind, maybe, for he's lived all alone in that great big house ever since. I guess it does him good to have you little girls for friends."

"What was his wife like?" asked Mabel, eagerly. "Did you use to know her?"

"No, indeed," said Mrs. Crane, again giving the objectionable sniff. "That is, not so very well—a little light-headed, useless thing, no more fit to keep house—but there! there. It doesn't make any difference now, and I've learned that it isn't the best housekeepers that get married easiest. If it was, I wouldn't be so worried now."

"Is anything the matter?" asked Jean, quick to note the distress in Mrs. Crane's voice.

"Yes," returned the good woman, "there are two things the matter."

"Your poor foot?" queried Bettie, instantly all sympathy.

"No, the foot's all right. It's Mr. Barlow and my eyes. Mr. Barlow is going to be married to a young lady he's been writing to for a long time, and I'm going to lose him because he wants to keep house. It won't be easy to find another lodger for that little, shabby, old-fashioned room. I'm trying to make a new rag carpet for it, but I'm all at a standstill because I can't see to thread my needle. I declare, I don't know what is going to become of me."

"When I grow up," said Bettie, "you shall live with me."

"But what am I to do while I'm waiting for you to grow up?" asked Mrs. Crane, smiling at Bettie's protecting manner.

"Let us be your eyes," suggested Jean. "Couldn't we thread about a million needles for you? Don't you think a million would last all day?"

"I should think it might," said Mrs. Crane, somewhat comforted. "I haven't quite a million, but if Marjory will get my cushion and a spool of cotton I'll be very glad to have you thread all I have."

The girls worked in silence for fully five minutes. Then Mabel jabbed the solitary needle she had threaded into the sawdust cushion and said:

"Don't you suppose Mr. Downing might let us have the cottage now, if we went to him? Nobody else seems to care about it. What do you think, Mrs. Crane?"

"Why, my dear, I suppose it wouldn't do any harm to ask. You'd better see what your own people think about it."

"Let's go ask them now," cried impetuous Mabel, springing to her feet. Forgetting all about the needles and without waiting to say good-by to Mrs. Crane, the eager girl made a diagonal rush for the corner nearest her own home.

The others remained long enough to thread all the needles. Then they, too, went home with the news about the cottage and about Mrs. Crane. They were realizing, for the first time, that their good friend might become helpless long before they were ready to use her as a grandmother for their children, but they couldn't see just what was to be done about it. The idea of going to Mr. Downing, however, soon drove every other thought away, for the parents and Aunty Jane, too, advised them to ask. They even encouraged them.

But when Jean and Bettie, hopefully dressed in their Sunday-best, and Marjory and Mabel, with their abundant locks elaborately curled besides, presented themselves and their request at Mr. Downing's house that evening, they were not at all encouraged by their reception.

Mr. Downing, a man of moods, had just come off second-best in an encounter with Mrs. Milligan, whom he had accidentally met on his way home to dinner, and, at the moment the girls appeared, the cottage was just about the last subject that the badgered man cared to discuss. Before Jean had fairly stated her errand, the enraged Mr. Downing roared "No!" so emphatically that his four alarmed visitors backed hurriedly off the Downing porch and fled as one girl. Mabel, to be sure, measured her length in the canna bed near the gate, but she scrambled up, snorting with fright and indignation, and none of them paused again in their flight until Jean's door, which seemed safest, had closed behind them.

CHAPTER 19.
THE RESPONSE TO
MABEL'S TELEGRAM

The night of their flitting from Dandelion Cottage, the girls had hastily eaten all the radishes in the cottage garden to prevent their falling into the hands of the grasping Milligans. Now, the morning after their visit to Mr. Downing, they were wishing that they hadn't; not because the radishes had disagreed with them, but for quite a different reason. They could not enter the cottage, of course, but it had occurred to them that it might be possible to derive a certain melancholy satisfaction from tending and replenishing the little garden. That pleasure, at least, had not been forbidden them; but before beginning active operations, they took the precaution of enlarging the hole in the back fence, so that instantaneous flight would be possible in case Mr. Downing should stroll cottageward.

Their motive was good. When Mr. Black returned, if he ever should, Bettie meant that he should find the little yard in perfect order.

"We'll keep to our part of the bargain, anyway," said Bettie, as the four girls were making their first cautious tour of inspection about the cottage yard. "There's lots of work to be done."

"Yes," agreed Jean. "We said we'd keep this yard nice all summer, and it wouldn't be right not to do it."

"I wonder if we ought to ask Mr. Downing?" asked conscientious Bettie, stooping to pull off some gone-to-seed pansies.

"Perhaps you'd like the job!" suggested Marjory, with mild sarcasm.

"My sakes!" said Mabel. "I wouldn't go near that man again if I was going to swallow an automobile the next moment if I didn't. I could hear him roar 'No' every few minutes all night. I fell out of bed twice, dreaming that I was trying to get off of that old porch of his before he could grab me."

"Well, I guess we'd better not ask," said Jean, "because I'm pretty sure he'd have the same answer ready."

"He certainly ought not to mind having us take care of our own flowers," said Marjory.

"That's true," said Bettie, poking the moist earth with a friendly finger. "They're growing splendidly since the rain. See how nice and full of growiness the ground is."

"I can get more pansy plants," offered Marjory, "to fill up these holes the Milligan dog made."

"Mrs. Crane promised to give us some aster plants," said Mabel. "Let's put 'em along by the fence."

"Let's do," said Jean. "You go see if you can have them now."

"I know Mr. Black will be pleased," declared Bettie, "if he finds this place looking nice. I'm so thankful we didn't remember to ask Mr. Downing about it."

"We didn't have a chance," said Jean, ruefully; "but just the same, I'm willing to keep on forgetting until Mr. Black comes."

It began to look, however, as if Mr. Black were never coming. Bettie had written as she had promised but had had no reply, though the letter had not been mailed for ten minutes before she began to watch for the postman. Even Mabel, having had no response to her telegram and supposing it to have gone astray, had given up hope.

Mabel, ever averse to confessing the failure of any of her enterprises, had decided to postpone saying anything about the telegram until one or another of the girls should remember to ask what had become of the thirty-five cents. So far, none of them had thought of it.

Still, it seemed probable, in spite of Mr. Black's continued absence, that he would get home some time, for he had left so much behind him. In the business portion of the town there was a huge building whose sign read: "peter black and company." Then, in the prettiest part of the residence district, where the lawns were big and the shrubs were planted scientifically by a landscape gardener and where the hillside bristled with roses, there was a large, handsome stone house that, as everybody knew, belonged to Mr. Black. Although there were industrious clerks at work in the one, and a middle-aged housekeeper, with a furnace-tending, grass-cutting husband equally busy in the other, it was reasonable to suppose that Mr. Black, even if he had no family, would have to return some time, if only to enjoy his beloved rose-bushes.

Thanks to Mabel's telegram (Bettie's letter, forwarded from Washington, did not reach him for many days) he did come. He had had to stop in Chicago, after all, and there had been unexpected delays; but just a week from the day the Milligans had left the cottage, Mr. Black returned.

Without even stopping to look in at his own office, the traveler went straight to the rectory to ask for Bettie. Bettie, Mrs. Tucker told him, he would probably find in the cottage yard.

Mr. Black took a short cut through the hole in the back fence, arriving on the cottage lawn just in time to meet a procession of girls entering the front gate. Each girl was carrying a huge, heavy clod of earth, out of the top of which grew a sturdy green plant; for the cottageless cottagers had discovered the only successful way of performing the difficult feat of restocking their garden with half-grown vegetables. Their neighbors had proved generous when Bettie had explained that if one could only dig deep enough one could transplant anything, from a cabbage to pole-beans. Some of the grown-up gardeners, to be sure, had been skeptical, but they were all willing that the girls should make the attempt.

"Oh, Mr. Black!" shrieked the four girls, dropping their burdens to make a simultaneous rush for the senior warden. "Oh! oh! oh! Is it really you? We're so glad—so awfully glad you've come!"

"Well, I declare! So am I," said Mr. Black, with his arms full of girls. "It seems like getting home again to have a family of nice girls waiting with a welcome, even if it's a pretty sandy one. What are you doing with all the real estate? I thought you'd all been turned out, but you seem to be all here. I declare, if you haven't all been growing!"

"We were—we are—we have," cried the girls, dancing up and down delightedly. "Mr. Downing made us give up the cottage, but he didn't say anything about the garden—and—and—we thought we'd better forget to ask about it."

"Tell me the whole story," said Mr. Black. "Let's sit here on the door-step. I'm sure I could listen more comfortably if there were not so many excited girls dancing on my best toes."

So Mr. Black, with a girl at each side and two at his feet, heard the story from beginning to end, and he seemed to find it much more amusing than the girls had at any time considered it. He simply roared with laughter when Bettie apologized about Bob and the tin.

"Well," said he, when the recital was ended, and he had shown the girls Mabel's telegram, and the thoroughly delighted Mabel had been praised and enthusiastically hugged by the other three, "I have heard of cottages with more than one key. Suppose you see, Bettie, if anything on this ring will fit that keyhole."

Three of the flat, slender keys did not, but the fourth turned easily in the lock. Bettie opened the door.

"Possession," said Mr. Black, with a twinkle in his eye, "is nine points of the law. You'd better go to work at once and move in and get to cooking; you see, there's a vacancy under my vest that nothing but that promised dinner party can fill. The sooner you get settled, the sooner I get that good square meal. Besides, if you don't work, you won't have an appetite for a great big box of candy that I have in my trunk."

"Oh," sighed Bettie, rubbing her cheek against Mr. Black's sleeve, "it seems too good to be true."

"What, the candy?" teased Mr. Black.

"No, the cottage," explained Bettie, earnestly. "Oh, I do hope winter will be about six months late this year to make up for this."

"Perhaps it'll forget to come at all," breathed Mabel, hopefully. "I'd almost be willing to skip Christmas if there was any way of stretching this summer out to February. Somebody please pinch me—I'm afraid I'm dreaming—Oh! ouch! I didn't say everybody."

By this time, of course, all the young housekeepers' relatives were deeply interested in the cottage. After living for a never-to-be-forgotten week with the four unhappiest little girls in town, all were eager to reinstate them in the restored treasure. The girls, having rushed home with the joyful news, were almost overwhelmed with unexpected offers of parental assistance. The grown-ups were not only willing but anxious to help. Then, too, the Mapes boys and the young Tuckers almost came to blows over who should have the honor of mending the roof with the bundles of shingles that Dr. Bennett insisted on furnishing. Marjory's Aunty Jane said that if somebody who could drive nails without smashing his thumb would mend the holes in the parlor floor she would give the girls a pretty ingrain carpet, one side of which looked almost new. Dr. Bennett himself laid a clean new floor in the little kitchen over the rough old one, and Mrs. Mapes mended the broken plaster in all the rooms by pasting unbleached muslin over the holes. Mr. Tucker replaced all broken panes of glass, while his busy wife found time to tack mosquito-netting over the kitchen and pantry windows.

So interested, indeed, were all the grown-ups and all the brothers that the girls chuckled delightedly. It wouldn't have surprised them so very much if all their people had fallen suddenly to playing with dolls and to having tea-parties in the cottage; but the place was still far too disorderly for either of these juvenile occupations to prove attractive to anybody.

In the midst of the confusion, Mr. Downing stopped at the cottage door one noon and asked for the girls, who eyed him doubtfully and resentfully as they met him, after Marjory had hesitatingly ushered him into the untidy little parlor.

Mr. Downing smiled at them in a friendly but decidedly embarrassed manner. He had not forgotten his own lack of cordiality when the girls had called on him, and he wanted to atone for it. Mr. Black had tactfully but effectively pointed out to Mr. Downing—already deeply disgusted with the Milligans—the error of his ways, and Mr. Downing, as generous as he was hasty and irascible, was honest enough to admit that he had been mistaken not only in his estimate of Mr. Black, but also in his treatment of the little cottagers. Now, eager to make amends, he looked somewhat anxiously from one to another of his silent hostesses, who in return looked questioningly at Mr. Downing. Surely, with Mr. Black in town, Mr. Downing couldn't be thinking of turning them out a second time; still, he had disappointed them before, probably he would again, and the girls meant to take no chances. So they kept still, with searching eyes glued upon Mr. Downing's countenance. All at once, they realized that they were looking into friendly eyes, and three of them jumped to the conclusion that the junior warden was not the heartless monster they had considered him.

"I came," said Mr. Downing, noticing the change of expression in Bettie's face, "to offer you, with my apologies, this key and this little document. The paper, as you will see, is signed by all the vestrymen—my own name is written very large—and it gives you the right to the use of this cottage until such time as the church feels rich enough to tear it down and build a new one. There is no immediate cause for alarm on this score, for there were only sixty-two cents in the plate last Sunday. I have come to the conclusion, young ladies, that I was overhasty in my judgment. I didn't understand the matter, and I'm afraid I acted without due consideration—I often do. But I hope you'll forgive me, for I sincerely beg all your pardons."

"It's all right," said Bettie, "as long as it was just a mistake. It's easy to forgive mistakes."

"Yes," said Marjory, sagely, "we all make 'em."

"It's all right, anyway," added Jean.

Mr. Downing looked expectantly at Mabel, who for once had preserved a dead silence.

"Well?" he asked, interrogatively.

"I don't suppose I can ever really quite forgive you," confessed Mabel, with evident reluctance. "It'll be awfully hard work, but I guess I can try."

"Perhaps my peace-offering will help your efforts a little," said Mr. Downing, smiling. "It seems to be coming in now at your gate."

The girls turned hastily to look, but all they could see was a very untidy man with a large book under his arm.

"These," said Mr. Downing, taking the book from the man, who had walked in at the open door, "are samples of inexpensive wall papers. You're to choose as much as you need of the kinds you like best, and this man will put it wherever it will do the most good, and I'll pay the bill. Now, Miss Blue Eyes, do I stand a better chance of forgiveness?"

"Yes, yes!" cried Mabel. "I'm almost glad you needed to apologize. You did it beautifully, too. Mercy, when I apologize—and I have to do a fearful lot of apologizing—I don't begin to do it so nicely!"

"Perhaps," offered Mr. Downing, "when you've had as much practice as I have, it will come easier. I see, however, that you are far more suitable tenants than the Milligans would have been, for my humble apologies to them met with a very different reception. I assure you that, if there's ever any rivalry between you again, my vote goes with you—you're so easily satisfied. Now don't hesitate to choose whatever you want from this book. This paperhanger is yours, too, until you're done with him."

"Oh, thank you, thank you, thank you," cried the girls, with happy voices, as Mr. Downing turned to go; "you couldn't have thought of a nicer peace-offering."

Of course it took a long, long time for so many young housekeepers to choose papers for the parlor and the two bedrooms, but after much discussion and many differences of opinion, it was finally selected. The girls decided on green for the parlor, blue for one bedroom, and pink for the other, and they were easily persuaded to choose small patterns.

Then the smiling paperhanger worked with astonishing rapidity and said that he didn't object in the least to having four pairs of bright eyes watch from the doorway every strip go into place. It seemed to be no trouble at all to paper the little low-ceilinged cottage, and, oh! how beautiful it was when it was all done. The cool, cucumber-green parlor was just the right shade to melt into the soft blue and white of the front bedroom. As for the dainty pink room, as Bettie said rapturously, it fairly made one smell roses to look at it, it was so sweet.

It was finished by the following night, for no paperhanger could have had the heart to linger over his work with so many anxious eyes following every movement. Mrs. Tucker washed and ironed and mended the white muslin curtains; and, with such a bower to move into, the second moving-in and settling, the girls decided, was really better than the first. When their belongings were finally reinstalled in the cottage even Mabel no longer felt resentful toward the Milligans.

CHAPTER 20.
THE ODD BEHAVIOR OF
THE GROWN-UPS

Even with all its ingenious though inexpensive improvements, the renovated cottage would probably have failed to satisfy a genuine rent-paying family, but to the contented girls it seemed absolutely perfect.

At last, it looked to everybody as if the long-deferred dinner party were actually to take place. There, in readiness, were the girls, the money, the cottage, and Mr. Black, and nothing had happened to Mrs. Bartholomew Crane—who might easily, as Mabel suggested harrowingly, have moved away or died at any moment during the summer.

One day, very soon after the cottage was settled, a not-at-all-surprised Mr. Black and a very-much-astonished Mrs. Crane each received a formal invitation to dine under its reshingled roof. Composed by all four, the note was written by Jean, whose writing and spelling all conceded to be better than the combined efforts of the other three. Bettie delivered the notes with her own hand, two days before the event, and on the morning of the party she went a second time to each house to make certain that neither of the expected guests had forgotten the date.

"Forget!" exclaimed Mr. Black, standing framed in his own doorway. "My dear little girl, how could I forget, when I've been saving room for that dinner ever since early last spring? Nothing, I assure you, could keep me away or even delay me. I have eaten a very light breakfast, I shall go entirely without luncheon—"

"I wouldn't do that," warned Bettie. "You see it's our first dinner party and something might go wrong. The soup might scorch—"

"It wouldn't have the heart to," said Mr. Black. "No soup could be so unkind."

Of course the cottage was the busiest place imaginable during the days immediately preceding the dinner party. The girls had made elaborate plans and their pockets fairly bulged with lists of things that they were to be sure to remember and not on any account to forget. Then the time came for them to begin to do all the things that they had planned to do, and the cottage hummed like a hive of bees.

First the precious seven dollars and a half, swelled by some mysterious process to seven dollars and fifty-seven cents, had to be withdrawn from the bank, the most imposing building in town with its almost oppressive air of formal dignity. The rather diffident girls went in a body to get the money and looked with astonishment at the extra pennies.

"That's the interest," explained the cashier, noting with quiet amusement the puzzled faces.

"Oh," said Jean, "we've had that in school, but this is the first time we've ever seen any."

"We didn't suppose," supplemented Bettie, "that interest was real money. I thought it was something like those x-plus-y things that the boys have in algebra."

"Or like mermaids and goddesses," said Mabel.

"She means myths," interpreted Marjory.

"I see," said the cashier. "Perhaps you like real, tangible interest better than the kind you have in school."

"Oh, we do, we do!" cried the four girls.

"After this," confided Bettie, "it will be easier to study about."

Then, with the money carefully divided into three portions, placed in three separate purses, which in turn were deposited one each in Jean's, Marjory's, and Bettie's pockets, Mabel having flatly declined to burden herself with any such weighty responsibility, the four went to purchase their groceries.

The smiling clerks at the various shops confused them a little at first by offering them new brands of breakfast foods with strange, oddly spelled names, but the girls explained patiently at each place that they were giving a dinner party, not a breakfast, and that they wanted nothing but the things on their list. It took time and a great deal of discussion to make so many important purchases, but finally the groceries were all ordered.

Next the little housekeepers went to the butcher's to ask for a chicken.

"Vat kind of schicken you vant?" asked the stout, impatient German butcher.

Jean looked at Bettie, Bettie looked at Marjory, and Marjory, although she knew it was hopeless, looked at Mabel.

"Vell?" said the busy butcher, interrogatively.

"One to cook—without feathers," gasped Jean.

"A spring schicken?"

"Is that—is that better than a summer one?" faltered Bettie, cautiously. "You see it's summer now."

"Perhaps," suggested Mabel, seized with a bright thought, "an August one"

"Here, Schon," shouted the busy butcher to his assistant, "you pring oudt three-four schicken. You can pick von oudt vile I vaits on dese odder gostomer."

"I think," said Jean, indicating one of the fowls John had produced for her inspection, "that that's about the right size. It's so small and smooth that it ought to be tender."

"I wouldn't take that one, Miss," cautioned honest John, under his breath, "it looks to me like a little old bantam rooster. Leave it to me and I'll find you a good one."

To his credit, John was as good as his word.

The little housekeepers felt very important indeed, when, later in the day, a procession of genuine grocery wagons, drawn by flesh-and-blood horses, drew up before the cottage door to deliver all kinds of really-truly parcels. They had not quite escaped the breakfast foods after all, because each consignment of groceries was enriched by several sample packages; enough altogether, the girls declared joyously, to provide a great many noon luncheons.

Of course all the parcels had to be unwrapped, admired, and sorted before being carefully arranged in the pantry cupboard, which had never before found itself so bountifully supplied. Then, for a busy half-day, cook books and real cooks were anxiously consulted; for, as Mabel said, it was really surprising to see how many different ways there were to cook even the simplest things.

Jean and Bettie were to do the actual cooking. The other two, in elaborately starched caps and aprons of spotless white (provided Mabel, though this seemed doubtful, could keep hers white), were to take turns serving the courses. The first course was to be tomato soup; it came in a can with directions outside and cost fifteen cents, which Mabel considered cheap because of the printed cooking lesson.

"If they'd send printed directions with their raw chickens and vegetables," said she, "maybe folks might be able to tell which recipe belonged to which thing."

"Well," laughed Marjory, "some cooks don't have to read a whole page before they discover that directions for making plum pudding don't help them to make corned-beef hash. You always forget to look at the top of the page."

"Never mind," said Jean, "she found a good recipe for salad dressing."

"That's true," said Marjory, "but before you use it you'd better make sure that it isn't a polish for hardwood floors. There, don't throw the book at me, Mabel—I won't say another word."

The three mothers and Aunty Jane, grown suddenly astonishingly obliging, not only consented to lend whatever the girls asked for, but actually thrust their belongings upon them to an extent that was almost overwhelming. The same impulse seemed to have seized them all. It puzzled the girls, yet it pleased them too, for it was such a decided novelty to have six parents (even the fathers appeared interested) and one aunt positively vying with one another to aid the young cottagers with their latest plan. The girls could remember a time, not so very far distant, when it was almost hopeless to ask for even such common things as potatoes, not to mention eggs and butter. Now, however, everything was changed. Aunty Jane would provide soup spoons, napkins, and a tablecloth—yes, her very best short one. Marjory could hardly believe her ears, but hastily accepted the cloth lest the offer should be withdrawn. The girls, having set their hearts on using the "Frog that would a-wooing go" plates for the escalloped salmon (to their minds there seemed to be some vague connection between frogs and fishes), were compelled to decline offers of all the fish plates belonging to the four families. The potato salad, garnished with lettuce from the cottage garden, was to be eaten with Mrs. Bennett's best salad forks The roasted chicken was not to be entrusted to the not-always-reliable cottage oven but was to be cooked at the Tuckers' house and carved with Mr. Mapes's best game set. Mrs. Bennett's cook would make a pie—yes, even a difficult lemon pie with a meringue on top, promised Mrs. Bennett.

Then there were to be butter beans out of the cottage garden, and sliced cucumbers from the green-grocer's because Mrs. Crane had confessed to a fondness for cucumbers. There was one beet in the garden almost large enough to be eaten; that, too, was to be sacrificed. The dessert had been something of a problem. It had proved so hard to decide this matter that they decided to compromise by adding both pudding and ice cream to the Bennett pie. A brick of ice cream and some little cakes could easily be purchased ready-made from the town caterer, with the change they had left. Thoughts of their money's giving out no longer troubled them, for had not Mabel's surprising father told them that if they ran short they need not hesitate to ask him for any amount within reason?

"I declare," said bewildered Mabel, "I can't see what has come over Papa and Mamma. Do I look pale, or anything—as if I might be going to die before very long?"

"No," said Marjory, "you certainly don't; but I've wondered if Aunty Jane could be worried about me. I never knew her to be so generous— why, it's getting to be a kind of nuisance! Do you s'pose they're going to insist on doing everything?"

"Well," said Bettie, "they've certainly helped us a lot. I don't know why they've done it, but I'm glad they have. You see, we must have everything perfectly beautiful because Mr. Black is rich and is accustomed to good dinners, and Mrs. Crane is poor and never has any very nice ones. If our people keep all their promises, it can't help being a splendid dinner."

The three mothers and Aunty Jane and all the fathers did keep their promises. They, too, wanted the dinner to be a success, for they knew, as all the older residents of the little town knew—and as the children themselves might have known if the story had not been so old and their parents had been in the habit of gossiping (which fortunately they were not)—that there was a reason why Mr. Black and Mrs. Crane were the last two persons to be invited to a tête-à-tête dinner party. Yet, strangely enough, there was an equally good reason why no one wanted to interfere and why everyone wanted to help.

CHAPTER 21.
THE DINNER

The girls, a little uneasy lest their alarmingly interested parents should insist on cooking and serving the entire dinner, were both relieved and perplexed to find that the grown-ups, while perfectly willing to help with the dinner provided they could work in their own kitchens, flatly declined the most urgent invitations to enter the cottage on the afternoon or evening of the party.

It was incomprehensible. Until noon of the very day of the feast the parents and Aunty Jane had paid the girls an almost embarrassing number of visits. Now, when the girls really wanted them and actually gave each of them a very special invitation, each one unexpectedly held aloof. For, as the hour approached, the girls momentarily became more and more convinced that something would surely go wrong in the cottage kitchen with no experienced person to keep things moving. They decided, at four o'clock, to ask Mrs. Mapes to oversee things.

"No, indeed," said Mrs. Mapes. "You may have anything there is in my house, but you can't have me. You don't need anybody; you won't have a mite of trouble."

Finding Mrs. Mapes unpersuadable, they went to Mrs. Tucker, who, next to Jean's mother, was usually the most obliging of parents.

"No," said Mrs. Tucker, "I couldn't think of it. No, no, no, not for one moment. It's much better for you to do it all by yourselves."

Still hopeful, the girls ran to Mrs. Bennett.

"Mercy, no!" exclaimed that good woman, with discouraging emphasis. "I'm not a bit of use in a strange kitchen, and there are reasons—Oh! I mean it's your party and it won't be any fun if somebody else runs it."

"Shall we ask your Aunty Jane?" asked Bettie. "We don't seem to be having any luck."

"Yes," replied Marjory. "She loves to manage things."

But Marjory's Aunty Jane proved no more willing than the rest.

"No, ma'am!" she said, emphatically. "I wouldn't do it for ten dollars. Why, it would just spoil everything to have a grown person around. Don't even think of such a thing."

So the girls, feeling just a little indignant at their disobliging relatives, decided to get along as well as they could without them.

At last, everything was either cooked or cooking. The table was beautifully set and decorated and flowers bloomed everywhere in Dandelion Cottage. Jean and Bettie, in the freshest of gingham aprons, were taking turns watching the things simmering on the stove. Mabel, looking fatter than ever in her short, white, stiffly starched apron, was on the doorstep craning her neck to see if the guests showed any signs of coming, and Marjory was busily putting a few entirely unnecessary finishing touches to the table.

The guests were invited for half-past six, but had been hospitably urged by Bettie to appear sooner if they wished. At exactly fifteen minutes after six, Mrs. Crane, in her old-fashioned, threadbare, best black silk and a very-much-mended real-lace collar, and with her iron-gray hair far more elaborately arranged than she usually wore it, crossed the street, lifting her skirts high and stepping gingerly to avoid the dust.

She supposed that she was to be the only guest, for the girls had not mentioned any other.

Mabel, prodigiously formal and most unusually solemn, met her at the door, ushered her into the blue room, and invited her to remove her wraps. The light shawl that Mrs. Crane had worn over her head was the only wrap she had, but it was not so easily removed as it might have been. It caught on one of her hair pins, which necessitated rearranging several locks of hair that had slipped from place. This took some time and, while she was thus occupied, Mr. Black turned the corner, went swiftly toward the cottage, mounted the steps, and rang the doorbell.

Mabel received him with even greater solemnity than she had Mrs. Crane.

"I think I'd better take your hat," said she. "We haven't any hat rack, but it'll be perfectly safe on the pink-room bed because we haven't any Tucker babies taking naps on it today."

Mr. Black handed his hat to her with an elaborate politeness that equaled her own.

"Marjory!" she whispered as she went through the dining-room. "He's wearing his dress suit!"

"Sh! he'll hear you," warned Marjory.

"Well, anyway, I'm frightened half to death. Oh, would you mind passing all the wettest things? I hadn't thought about his clothes."

"Yes, I guess I'd better; he might want to wear 'em again."

"They're both here," announced Mabel, opening the kitchen door.

"You help Bettie stir the soup and the mashed potatoes," said Jean, whisking off her apron and tying it about Mabel's neck. "I'll go in and shake hands with them and then come back and dish up."

Jean found both guests looking decidedly ill at ease. Mr. Black stood by the parlor table absent-mindedly undressing a family of paper dolls. Mrs. Crane, pale and nervously clutching the curtain, seemed unable to move from the bedroom doorway.

"Oh!" said Jean, "I do believe Mabel forgot all about introducing you. We told her to be sure to remember, but she hasn't been able to take her mind off of her apron since she put it on. Mrs. Crane, this is our—our preserver, Mr. Black."

The guests bowed stiffly.

Jean began to wish that she could think of some way to break the ice. Both were jolly enough on ordinary occasions, but apparently both had suddenly been stricken dumb. Perhaps dinner parties always affected grown persons that way, or perhaps the starch from Mabel's apron had proved contagious; Jean smiled at the thought. Then she made another effort to promote sociability.

"Mrs. Crane," explained Jean, turning to Mr. Black, who was nervously tearing the legs off of the father of the paper-doll family, "is our very nicest neighbor. We like her just ever so much—everybody does. We've often told you, Mrs. Crane, how fond we are of Mr. Black. It was because you are our two very dearest friends that we invited you both—"

"Je-e-e-e-an!" called a distressed voice from the kitchen.

"Mercy!" exclaimed Jean, making a hurried exit, "I hope that soup isn't scorched!"

"No," said Bettie, slightly aggrieved, "but I wanted a chance, too, to say how-do-you-do to those people before I get all mixed up with the cooking. I thought you were never coming back."

"Well, it's your turn now," said Jean. "Give me that spoon."

Bettie, finding their guests seated in opposite corners of the room and apparently deeply interested in the cottage literature—Mr. Black buried in Dottie Dimple and Mrs. Crane absorbed in Mother Goose—naturally concluded that they were waiting to be introduced, and accordingly made the presentation.

"Mrs. Crane," said she, "I want you to meet Mr. Black, and I hope," added warm-hearted Bettie, "that you'll like each other very much because we're so fond of you both. You're each a surprise party for the other—we thought you'd both like it better if you had somebody besides children to talk to."

"Very kind, I'm sure," mumbled Mr. Black, whose company manners, it seemed to Bettie, were far from being as pleasant as his everyday ones. Bettie gave a deep sigh and made one more effort to set the conversational ball rolling.

"I'm afraid I'll have to go back to the kitchen now, and leave you to entertain each other. Please both of you be very entertaining—you're both so jolly when you just run in."

Bettie's eyes were wistful as she went toward the kitchen. Was it possible, she wondered, that her beloved Mr. Black could despise Mrs. Crane because she was poor? It didn't seem possible, yet there was certainly something wrong. Perhaps he was merely hungry. That was it, of course; she would put the dinner on at once—even good-natured Dr. Tucker, she remembered, was sometimes a little bearlike when meals were delayed.

Five minutes later, Marjory escorted the guests to the dining-room, and, finding both of these usually talkative persons alarmingly silent, she inferred of course that Mabel had forgotten—as indeed Mabel had—her instructions in regard to introducing them. Marjory's manners on formal occasions were very pretty; they were pretty now, and so was she, as she hastened to make up for Mabel's oversight.

"Oh, Mr. Black," she cried, earnestly, "I'm afraid no one remembered to introduce you. It's our first dinner party, you know, and we're not very wise. This is our dearest neighbor, Mrs. Crane, Mr. Black."

The guests bowed stiffly for the third time. Practice should have lent grace to the salutation, but seemingly it had not.

"Aren't some of you young people going to sit down with me?"

demanded Mr. Black, noticing suddenly that the table was set for only two.

"Yes," said Mrs. Crane with evident dismay, "surely you're coming to the table, too."

"We can't," explained Marjory. "It takes all of us to do the serving. Besides, we haven't but two dining-room chairs. Sit here, please, Mrs. Crane; and this is your place, Mr. Black."

Mr. Black looked red and uncomfortable as he unfolded his napkin. Mrs. Crane looked, as Marjory said afterward, for all the world as if she were going to cry. Perhaps the prospect of a good dinner after a long siege of poor ones was too much for her, for ordinarily Mrs. Crane was a very cheerful woman.

Although both guests declared that the soup was very good indeed, neither seemed to really enjoy it.

"They just kind of worried a little of it down," said the distressed Marjory, when she handed Mr. Black's plate, still three-quarters full, to Jean in the kitchen. "Do you suppose there's anything the matter with it?"

"There can't be," said Bettie. "I've tasted it and it's good."

"They're just saving room for the other things," comforted Mabel. "I guess I wouldn't fill myself up with soup if I could smell roasted chicken keeping warm in the oven."

Although Mabel had asked to be spared passing the spillable things, it seemed reasonably safe to trust her with the dish of escalloped salmon. She succeeded in passing it without disaster to either the dish or the guests' garments, and her apron was still immaculate.

"Why," exclaimed Mabel, suddenly noticing that the guests sat stiff and silent, "the girls said I was to be sure to introduce you the moment you came, and I never thought a thing about it. Do forgive me—I'm the stupidest girl. Mrs. Black—I mean Mr. Crane—no, Mrs. Crane—"

"We've been introduced," said Mr. Black, rather shortly. "Might I have a glass of water?"

A pained, surprised look crept into Mabel's eyes. A moment later she went to the kitchen.

The instant the guests were left alone, Mrs. Crane did an odd thing. She leaned forward and spoke in a low, earnest tone to Mr. Black.

"Peter," she said, "can't we pretend to be sociable for a little while? It isn't comfortable, of course, but it isn't right to spoil those children's pleasure by acting like a pair of wooden dolls. Let's talk to each other whenever they're in the room just as if we had just met for the first time."

"You're right, Sarah," said Mr. Black. "Let's talk about the weather. It's a safe topic and there's always plenty of it."

When Marjory opened the door to carry in the salad there was a pleasant hum of voices in the dining-room. It seemed to all the girls that the guests were really enjoying themselves, for Mr. Black was telling Mrs. Crane how much warmer it was in Washington, and Mrs. Crane was informing Mr. Black that, except for the one shower that fell so opportunely on the Milligans, it had been a remarkably dry summer. The four anxious hostesses, feeling suddenly cheered, fell joyously to eating the soup and the salmon that remained on the stove. Until that moment, they had been too uneasy to realize that they were hungry; but as Marjory carried in the crackers, half-famished Mabel breathed a fervent hope that the guests wouldn't help themselves too lavishly to the salad.

To the astonishment of Mabel, who carried the chicken successfully to its place before Mr. Black, who was to carve it, Mr. Black did not ask the other guest what part she liked best, but, with a whimsical smile, quietly cut off both wings and put them on Mrs. Crane's plate.

Mrs. Crane looked up with an odd, tremulous expression—sort of weepy, Mabel called it afterwards—and said: "Thank you, Peter."

It seemed to Mabel at the time that the guests were getting acquainted with a rapidity that was little short of remarkable—"Peter" indeed.

Then, when everything else was eaten, and Marjory had brought the nuts and served them, Mrs. Crane, hardly waiting for the door to close behind the little waitress, leaned forward suddenly and said:

"Peter, do you remember how you pounded my thumb when I held that hard black walnut for you to crack?"

"I remember everything, Sarah. I've always been sorry about that thumb—and I've been sorry about a good many other things since. Do you think—do you think you could forgive me?"

"Well, I just guess I could," returned Mrs. Crane, heartily. "After all, it was just as much my fault as it was yours—maybe more."

"No, I never thought that, Sarah. I was the one to blame."

When the door opened a moment later to admit the finger-bowls and all four of the girls, who had licked the ice-cream platter and had nothing more to do in the kitchen since everything had been served—there, to the housekeepers' unbounded amazement, were Mr. Black and Mrs. Crane, with their arms stretched across the little table, holding each other's middle-aged hands in a tight clasp, and both had tears in their eyes.

The girls looked at them in consternation.

"Was—was it the dinner?" ventured Mabel, at last. "Was it as bad as—as all that?"

"Well," said Mr. Black, rising to go around the table to place an affectionate arm across Mrs. Crane's plump shoulders, "it was the dinner, but not its badness—or even its very goodness."

"I guess you'd better tell 'em all about it, Peter," suggested Mrs. Crane, whose eyes were shining happily. "It's only fair they should know about it—bless their little hearts."

"Well, you see," said Mr. Black, who, as the girls had quickly discovered, was once more their own delightfully jolly friend, "once upon a time, a long time ago, there was a black-eyed girl named Sarah, and a two-years-younger boy, who looked a good deal like her, named Peter, and they were brother and sister. They were all the brothers and sisters that each had, for their parents died when this boy and girl were very young. Peter and Sarah used to dream a beautiful dream of living together always, and of going down hand-in-hand to a peaceful, plentiful old age. You see, they had no other relative but one very cross grandmother, who scolded them both even oftener than they deserved—which was probably quite often enough. So I suspect that those abused, black-eyed, half-starved children loved each other more than most brothers and sisters do."

"Yes," agreed Mrs. Crane, nodding her head and smiling mistily, "they certainly did. The poor young things had no one else to love."

"That," said Mr. Black, "was no doubt the reason why, when the headstrong boy grew up and married a girl that his sister didn't like, and the equally headstrong girl grew up and married a man that her brother couldn't like—a regular scoundrel that—"

"Peter!" warned Mrs. Crane.

"Well," said Mr. Black, hastily, "it's all over now, and perhaps we had better leave that part of it out. It isn't a pretty story, and we'll never mention it again, Sarah. But anyway, girls, this foolish brother and sister quarreled, and the brothers-in-law and sisters-in-law and even the grandmother, who was old enough to know better, quarreled, until finally all four of those hot-tempered young persons were so angry that the brother named Peter said he'd never speak to his sister again, and the sister named Sarah said she'd never speak to her brother again—and they haven't until this very day. Just a pair of young geese, weren't they, Sarah?"

"Old geese, too," agreed Mrs. Crane, "for they've both been fearfully lonely ever since and they've both been too proud to say so. One of them, at least, has wished a great many times that there had never been any quarrel."

"Two of 'em. But now this one," said Mr. Black, placing his forefinger against his own broad chest, "is going to ask this one—" and he pointed to Mrs. Crane—"to come and live with him in his own great big empty house, so he'll have a sister again to sew on his buttons, listen to his old stories, and make a home for him. What do you say, Sarah?"

"I say yes," said Mrs. Crane; "yes, with all my heart."

"And here," said Mr. Black, smiling into four pairs of sympathetic eyes, "are four young people who will have to pretend that they truly belong to us once in a while, because we'd both like to have our house full of happy little girls. You never had any children, Sarah?"

"No, and you lost your only one, Peter."

"Yes, a little brown-eyed thing like Bettie here—she'd be a woman now, probably with children of her own."

"It's—it's just like a story," breathed Bettie, happily. "We've been part of a real story and never knew it! I'm so glad you let us have Dandelion Cottage, so glad we invited you to dinner, and that nothing happened to keep either of you away."

"Peter and I are glad, too," said Mrs. Crane, who indeed looked wonderfully happy.

"Yes," said Mr. Black, "it's the most successful dinner party I've ever attended. Of course I can't hope to equal it, but as soon as Sarah and I get to keeping house properly and have decided which is to pour the coffee, we're going to return the compliment with a dinner that will make your eyes stick out, aren't we, Sarah?"

"Oh, we'll do a great deal more than that," responded generous Mrs. Crane. "We'll keep four extra places set at our table all the time."

"Of course we will," cried Mr. Black, heartily. "And we'll fill the biggest case in the library with children's books—we'll all go tomorrow to pick out the first shelfful—so that when it gets too cold for you to stay in Dandelion Cottage you'll have something to take its place. You're going to be little sunny Dandelions in the Black-Crane house whenever your own people can spare you. But what's the matter? Have you all lost your tongues? I didn't suppose you could be so astonishingly quiet."

"Oh," sighed Bettie, joyfully, "you've taken such a load off our minds. We were simply dreading the winter, with no cottage to have good times in."

"Yes," said Jean. "We didn't know how we could manage to live with the cottage closed. We've been wondering what in the world we were going to do."

"But with school, and you dear people to visit every day on the way home," said Marjory, "we'll hardly have time to miss it. Oh! won't it be perfectly lovely?"

"I'm going to begin at once to practice being on time to meals," said Mabel. "I'm not going to let that extra place do any waiting for me."

These were the things that the four girls said aloud; but the joyous look that flashed from Jean to Bettie, from Bettie to Marjory, from Marjory to Mabel, and from Mabel back again to Jean, said even more plainly: "Now there'll be somebody to take care of Mrs. Crane. Now there'll be somebody to make a home for lonely Mr. Black."

And indeed, subsequent events proved that it was a beautiful arrangement for everybody, besides being quite the most astonishing thing that had happened in the history of Lakeville.